ANN EVANS first started writing for her parish magazine, and went on to write scripts for her children's school pantomimes (she even played the back end of a cow in one of them!).

She is now a successful children's author, as well as an award-winning feature-writer on the *Coventry Evening Telegraph*. She divides her days between writing mystery and suspense novels for young readers, and non-fiction articles on a whole range of different topics – from animals to antiques – for various magazines and journals.

She was inspired to write thrillers set in the haunted Valley of Shadows after holidaying in Scotland, where she noticed how the light over the lochs can play tricks on your eyes...

RAMPAGE

Ann Evans

USBORNE

For Rob Tysall, thank you for all your support and
encouragement.

First published in the UK in 2008 by Usborne Publishing Ltd., Usborne
House, 83-85 Saffron Hill, London EC1N 8RT, England. www.usborne.com

A CIP catalogue record for this book is available from the British Library.

JFM MJJASOND/08 ISBN 9780746078921 Printed in Great Britain.

prologue

Giant metal teeth ripped the earth apart. Bulldozers painted yellow, and caked in mud, growled and trundled up and down great mounds of earth, raising and lowering the cutting edge of their steel buckets to slice into the wet ground for their next mouthful of clay and soil.

Huge chunks of mud, littered with thistles, bracken, tree roots and rocks were lifted up and held aloft like trophies in the jaws of these powerful machines. Then, with lights flashing, the bulldozers swivelled on their caterpillar tracks and rumbled up the growing mountains of earth, to deposit their loads.

The action was repetitive, and the sludging, slithering sound of metal blades against wet clay jarred against the monotonous growl of machinery. It was a noise that echoed uncannily through the peaceful Highland valleys and mountains.

The landscape was changing. But just a couple of kilometres or so away from this turmoil, the majestic Endrith Mountain stood as solid as ever. Endrith Valley – nicknamed the Valley of Shadows – was to remain intact, but the tiny roads and lanes nearby were undergoing a fierce transformation.

Construction of the Endrith bypass was well under way. The new dual carriageway would make driving to the northernmost tips of Scotland easier and swifter. But conservationists had warned that Endrith Valley must not be spoiled.

The loch and forest were beauty spots and the valley was steeped in history.

The new road would eventually be good for the area. But for now, it was a mess of noise and turmoil.

The late October drizzle deepened the colours of the clay, as the heavy machinery ploughed through it. The rain made the bare earth shine, so that the layers of dark red and orange were bright, the black and blue veins that streaked through the clay showing the depth of centuries that had passed.

Overhead the grey sky was heavy. Mist and cloud shrouded the mountains and the air was thick with the smells of diesel oil and mud. Workmen, in sturdy oilskin coats, hard hats and boots, slithered in the puddles. Some held walkie-talkie radios to make themselves heard above the chaos.

Andy Flintstock sat high up in the cabin of his bulldozer, expertly working the hydraulic controls, as he forged ahead with the new road. His metal trough swept down into the earth to grab another great mouthful of clay. But as he raised the full bucket, something caught his eye – something long and curved, protruding from the mass of soil in his trough. He peered out through his mud-streaked windscreen, but before he could figure out what it was, his bulldozer began to shake violently.

"What the...?"

He gripped his seat and braced himself, trying desperately not to be thrown about like a rag doll, but it was impossible. He was jerked roughly one way then the other as the massive earth-moving machine shook uncontrollably.

Instinctively he turned off the ignition – stopping the engine and the hydraulics – but the violent shaking went on.

Then, as suddenly as it had started, it stopped. Everything settled.

For a long heart-thudding moment Andy sat stock still, his eyes huge, staring at the raindrops trickling down his windscreen. He hardly dared breathe. Hardly dared move in case he started the whole thing shaking again.

"Andy! Andy what's going on?" Joe, his supervisor, yelled up as he came striding over.

Slowly, Andy released his grip on the controls, aware that beads of sweat were trickling down his face, just like the raindrops on his windows.

Trembling, he climbed down from his cabin. The cold drizzle on his face had never felt so good. "You tell me! That scared the life out of me!"

"What did you think you were playing at?" demanded Joe, glaring accusingly at Andy. "The thing almost toppled over sideways."

Andy looked flabbergasted. "*I* didn't make it do anything! The whole thing just started shaking. It must have been an earth tremor or something."

"Well I didn't feel anything," Joe said, frowning. "And it'd have to have been one heck of an earth tremor to move your bulldozer that much. Looked to me like you were messing around."

"Of course I wasn't!" Andy exclaimed, offended. "Why would I try to flip the thing over? I was scared out of my wits."

Joe raised his eyebrows, as if he wasn't sure

what to believe, then he strode over to the bulldozer's trough. "And what's this you've dug up?"

"I don't know. I was trying to get a look at it when everything went crazy," Andy grumbled, following Joe to the front of the bulldozer. He had to stand on tiptoes to see into the huge mechanical bucket, where the weird object was sticking out of the scooped-up mud.

It was long and curved and blackened with age. Andy reached in and scraped away some of the slimy clay that clung to it. For a moment he forgot the shock of the tremor, or whatever it was, as curiosity over this *thing* took its place.

"It's a bone, I'd say," murmured Joe. "An ancient old bone."

Andy shuddered as he felt the chill of it against his skin. "It's huge!" he whispered. "Do you think it's a dinosaur bone?"

Joe didn't answer. He was peering down into the hole in the ground left by the bulldozer's scoop. Looking back at Andy he quietly said, "Well, whatever it is...there's another one!"

* * *

On Endrith Mountain's highest ridge, an invisible presence stirred. A presence so powerful that it had endured and survived over thousands of years. Eons had passed, yet it remained, locked between two worlds. A presence that wasn't alive – but neither was it dead.

A spirit, existing in a mortal world.

As it lay enveloped now in the deepest of sleeps, a tremor touched the spirit's world. It stirred, restlessly. Although it did not wake, a low, silent growl drifted out across the valley.

An eagle, perched unwittingly on the same ridge, blinked in fright, sensing unseen danger. Instantly it spread wide its golden feathered wings and soared out from its lofty resting place. It glided effortlessly over the valley – away from the invisible threat.

Now on the rocky ledge, tiny specks of grit and dust began to move as if a spiralling current of wind was shifting them. But their movement had nothing to do with the wind. It was caused by a restless spirit locked in a world where it no longer belonged.

A spirit that belonged to a far distant time – a time when men lived in caves.

The spirit of the beast.

chapter one

four weeks later

Jack MacDonald peered over his dad's shoulder at the computer screen. His dad, expert palaeontologist, Professor Douglas MacDonald, was going through a disc of photographs that had been taken at the excavation site a kilometre or so down the road.

Since the bones had been discovered a month ago, work had stopped on the construction of the

Endrith bypass while a team of palaeontologists and volunteers, headed by Jack's dad, had moved in. They'd been granted a two-month period to excavate as much as they could from the area where the bones had been found. After that, construction of the road had to continue.

The discovery of ancient relics had brought in experts and scientists from all around the world. And today, now that the massive find had been almost completely uncovered, a television crew had turned up at the site to film the huge fossilized skeleton.

First thoughts that it was a dinosaur skeleton had been swiftly quashed once the experts had moved in. The long, curved bones measured four metres long. Only they weren't bones at all. They were tusks.

"I can't believe it's a real mammoth!" said Jack excitedly, studying the image on screen of what looked like an elephant's skull.

"I'd say it's a tundra mammoth, also known as a woolly mammoth," murmured his dad, zooming in on the image. "But there's never been a mammoth of any sort found in Scotland before now. The nearest was discovered in England, others in Ireland and Europe, then further afield in Siberia, North America, Alaska." He glanced up at Jack and his bearded face lit up. "It's one glorious discovery right on our doorstep, son."

"Amazing! A woolly mammoth, right here in Endrith!" exclaimed Jack, his brown eyes sparkling. Ancient history fascinated him. He'd been on loads of digs with his dad, but he'd never seen anything as exciting as this. "How old do you reckon it is then, Dad?"

"Well, mammoths were around for an incredibly long time. They roamed this planet anything from 150,000 to 5,000 years ago. But this one, I'd say, is only about 10,000 to 12,000 years old. And it's a pretty unusual specimen."

"Why's that?" Jack asked, gazing into the mammoth's eye socket, where a worm had been caught on camera just wriggling out.

"Because of its size," replied his dad, clicking onto the next image of what looked like a ribcage. "Mammoths in general ranged from two-and-a-half metres tall to four-and-a-half metres, about the size of an Asian elephant. But this monster was almost six metres in height – he was an absolute giant."

"How come he grew so big?" Jack asked, but his mum popped her head around the study door before his dad could answer.

"Quick, Douglas, you're on the television!"

They all dashed into the lounge and, sure enough, there was Jack's dad, filmed earlier that day at the excavation site.

The TV presenter was speaking to the camera, microphone in hand. "I'm just outside the Scottish town of Endrith, close to Endrith Valley – or the Valley of Shadows as the locals call it, because of rumours that it's haunted. And here a quite incredible event has occurred," he reported. "Work stopped on the construction of the Endrith bypass some four weeks ago, when the bones of what turned out to be an extinct woolly mammoth were unearthed. Since then, scientists from around the world have descended upon this peaceful area of the Highlands to take part in the excavation of this very rare discovery. We have with us now, Professor Douglas MacDonald of Edinburgh University, who actually lives close to the excavation site." He turned to Douglas. "So, professor, how exciting is this discovery to archaeologists, and basically, to the world at large?"

"Immensely exciting..." Jack's dad began. "But can I just point out that I'm not an archaeologist, I'm a palaeontologist. Archaeologists only study human history. We palaeontologists study other life forms..."

Jack and his mum started giggling.

"Dad!" Jack wailed. "Did you have to wear that hat while you were being filmed? You look a right geek!"

"Well I think I look quite intelligent," his dad huffed.

Heather MacDonald slid her arm around her husband and rested her auburn head on his shoulder. "Well you certainly sound it, dear."

They turned their attention back to the TV screen. "Experts are now carefully removing all the skeletal remains," Jack's dad was saying, leaning awkwardly towards the microphone. "They'll be taken to Edinburgh University, radiocarbon dated, and later they'll be reassembled. The skeleton will eventually be displayed at the Natural History Museum in London."

A helicopter had filmed the excavation site from above. It looked down into the massive crater where the outline of a mammoth lying on its side could clearly be seen.

"Wow! Look at that!" Jack gasped, staring at the images on the television. "It's fantastic!"

"Isn't it just!" agreed his dad, his eyes glued to the screen too. "I knew it was an almost totally complete mammoth specimen, but it's hard to take it in until you see it from above. This is going to put the find at Whitestone River in the shade."

"What's that about Whitestone River?" asked Jack's mum.

The professor answered without taking his eyes from the TV. "It's one of the best-preserved mammoth skeletons ever found...or rather it was. It was discovered in Canada, almost a complete skeleton. Carbon dating showed it to be around 30,000 years old. Ours is much younger – just a baby by comparison."

"Some baby!" murmured Jack's mum.

The interviewer was asking more questions. "Professor MacDonald, Endrith Valley has something of a reputation, has it not, for hauntings and ancient battle sounds. There was even a reported sighting of the ghost of a sabre-toothed tiger around eighteen months ago. The press nicknamed it 'the beast'. What do you make of all that?"

The professor gave a little laugh. "I can't really comment on that. True enough, some people believe they've heard battle sounds on the anniversary of the Battle of Endrith, a battle which took place in the Middle Ages. Others think they've been stalked by the ghost of a sabre-toothed tiger. But I've never experienced anything supernatural myself despite living here all my life. I prefer to stick to factual evidence, and these skeletal remains are hard proof that mammoths once lived in this country."

The camera rolled back to reveal a team of people on their knees in the excavation crater, delicately brushing soil from bones and placing them in trays. The presenter finished by reminding viewers that, in a year or two's time, the mammoth's skeleton would be displayed in the Natural History Museum for all to see.

Jack's mum heaved a sigh. "That's sad, don't you think?"

"Sad?" said Jack's dad, looking astonished. "It's incredible!"

Heather MacDonald pulled a face. "You would say that. Your job is to dig up bones. But I feel that when something is laid to rest, it should stay there."

"It's a prehistoric mammoth!" the professor chuckled, giving his wife a hug.

"Exactly!" she agreed. "It's been dead for thousands of years. Now, not only has its burial place been disturbed, but it's going to be put on display – it's so undignified. It's a shame it can't be left in peace."

"It's history, Mum," Jack groaned. "The whole world will want to see this!"

"He's right," said the professor. "This is the most exciting find in decades – if not *ever*. People will be clamouring to see this. It's astounding."

The TV was showing one last view from above. Jack was mesmerized. No wonder they called them mammoths – it *was* mammoth. And even though its bones were still clotted with mud, the shape was obvious. It almost looked like it was still running – the angle of its head and its legs just so...as if it had been charging along and then suddenly dropped down dead.

In death it looked awesome. In life it must have been unstoppable.

Jack was on his own computer, looking up woolly mammoths on the internet, when Cameron Kirk, his best mate from school, poked his head around the bedroom door. There were raindrops on his black-rimmed glasses and the light brown hair poking from beneath his hooded jacket was damp.

"Hiya! Your mum said to come up."

"Hi, Cameron! I'm just researching mammoths."

"That's what I've been doing. Isn't it amazing...a complete woolly mammoth skeleton, right here on our own doorstep! Some had long white hair y'know." He pulled up a chair next to Jack's at the computer desk. Although they were both fourteen, Cameron was a month younger than Jack. He had pale blue eyes and masses of freckles. "Saw your dad on the telly. D'you think he'd give me his autograph?"

"Probably! So don't ask," Jack groaned, scrolling down the screen to discover that the longest mammoth tusk on record was just over five point two metres long. "My dad thinks it's a giant tundra mammoth. I wonder if its tusks will break the tusk length record."

"A *giant* tundra mammoth? So how big is it?"

"About a metre taller than anything else that's ever been discovered. And my dad thinks it could be about 12,000 years old," Jack added. "Y'know what? I've just *got* to see it for myself, before it's taken off in plastic bags." He jumped to his feet.

"I'm gonna ask Dad if I can go to the site with him tomorrow. He usually lets me go with him. I found some really cool fossils last time, remember?"

Cameron's pale eyes lit up behind his spectacles. "Hey, can I come too? The TV cameras might be back – we might get on the telly!"

Jack grinned. "Let's go ask him."

Downstairs in his study, Douglas MacDonald's grey eyes shifted from one boy to the other as they stood eagerly in front of him, awaiting his decision. He leaned back in his chair, hands clasped behind his head, before he finally said, "It's exceptionally muddy down at the site. Cameron, you'd better check with your mother."

"Oh, she won't mind me getting a bit mucky, Mr. MacDonald," Cameron said earnestly, shuffling from foot to foot and looking hopefully from the professor to Jack.

Douglas sat pondering for a few more moments before coming to a decision. "Well, it is Saturday tomorrow, and we've really got to crack on with this excavation, so I suppose the more the merrier. After all, those roadworks won't wait for ever."

"So we can come?" Jack beamed. "Great! What do you want us to do?"

"Well, primarily, not to break anything!" answered his dad. "We're in the process of removing sections of the skeleton and getting the bones off to the university. You could help bag up the specimens, providing you don't mess around."

"Oh! We won't, Mr. MacDonald," Cameron promised solemnly. "You can count on us, we'll be really, really careful... Hey, I don't suppose you've unearthed any other bones have you...like maybe a sabre-toothed tiger's? When I first heard that two long, curved bones had been dug up, I was positive they'd be the sabre fangs of the beast."

"Not you as well, Cameron," groaned the professor. "The TV presenter harped on about that too. Why is it that people are more interested in the unknown than in actual facts?"

"But it *is* a fact that two kids were stalked by the ghost of a sabre-toothed tiger last year,"

Cameron stated. "It was in the paper. They said the beast manifested itself until they could see it really clearly, and it even attacked them." He turned his attention to Jack. "Manifestation, Jack, means taking on a living form, flesh and blood—"

"Becoming real." Jack nodded indulgently. "I know what manifestation means, Cam, I just don't believe in it!"

"Those children were delusional," Professor MacDonald said, dismissively. "Too much sun. It was a particularly hot summer if you remember, Cameron. The boy probably had sunstroke and was hallucinating...or just making the whole thing up."

"Those ghostbusters believed it," Cameron cheerfully argued on. "I read about some psychic research group coming here from York to track the beast down."

"But they didn't find it, did they?" Jack reminded his pal. "Cameron, you're so gullible when it comes to ghosts and stuff. The paranormal and psychic phenomena are just a load of old rubbish! When someone comes up with cold, hard evidence that the beast exists, then me and Dad might believe it. Till then, I'd say there's more chance of the Loch Ness Monster being real."

"Nessy probably does exist!" Cameron said earnestly. "You wouldn't be surprised if there were prehistoric fish or eels still living in the deepest lochs, would you, Mr. MacDonald?"

"It's not beyond the realms of possibility," agreed Jack's dad, stroking his bearded chin. "But that's not paranormal. If Nessy is around, then she's alive and kicking – a remnant from a long time ago, maybe, but a *living* remnant. Not a ghost."

"But people *have* seen ghosts!" Cameron went on, his pale eyes sparkling. "That psychic researcher woman who came here looking for the beast, for example, she ended up witnessing the Battle of Endrith – seven hundred years after it happened! I found their website. She'd drawn pictures of the ghostly warriors and everything – and they check out with everything historians already know."

"So what was to stop her doing a bit of research first?" The professor smiled, leaving the question hanging in mid-air for Cameron to think about. "Anyway these skeletal remains do at least prove that Scotland had woolly mammoths in prehistoric times. And who's to say we didn't have sabre-toothed tigers as well? I'm just not convinced their spirits are still sneaking around!"

"Aye, well I'm pretty convinced that there's something mysterious going on in the Valley of Shadows," Cameron said. "But I think discovering the mammoth is fantastic too. Oh, by the way, I saw you on the telly, Mr. MacDonald. You looked pretty cool."

"Thank you, Cameron. My son here thought I looked a bit of a geek."

"It was that hat, Dad." Jack grinned.

"You'll be glad of yours tomorrow, it's going to be cold, wet and muddy," the professor reminded them. "You'll also want wellingtons and warm waterproofs. And I want you ready for the off at eight o'clock sharp."

Jack's mum appeared with mugs of hot

chocolate. "Did I hear right? You boys are going on the dig?"

"Aye! It'll be brilliant," exclaimed Cameron, holding the door open for her. "You should come and see it too."

"Nah, Mum won't come," said Jack, taking two mugs from her tray and handing one to his pal. "Mum reckons we ought to let the mammoth rest in peace."

"Really? Why's that, Mrs. MacDonald? It's an amazing discovery."

"Yes, I know that," she said, handing her husband a drink. "But I just think it's sad – digging the poor creature up then dragging it away in pieces. I wouldn't be happy if it was me."

Jack flashed a sympathetic smile. "Mum, it's dead! It's been dead for thousands of years. It's nothing but a pile of old bones. What difference does it make where they're put?"

"Oh, drink your chocolate." She dismissed him with a wave of her hand. "You're just like your father. You just love those dry old relics, don't you!"

"And you're an old softy," said the professor, winking at the boys. "You know, if the mammoth was alive today, she'd be putting down a saucer of milk for it."

"I don't think so!" Jack's mum exclaimed, heading back to the kitchen. "If it was alive today, I'd be running for the hills."

chapter two

A layer of early morning mist shrouded the distant mountain peaks as Jack and Cameron climbed into Douglas MacDonald's four-wheel drive. But the dull, cloudy weather couldn't put a damper on either boy's mood.

"Got plenty of warm layers on, lads?" asked Jack's dad as he put the vehicle into gear.

"Snug as a bug, Mr. MacDonald," said

Cameron, sitting bolt upright in the back seat. "I've brought wellingtons for the dig, and a woolly hat – it's a bit like yours actually."

Jack and his dad exchanged glances but said nothing as they drove past the row of grey stone cottages. Jack lived at one end of the street, Cameron lived at the other. It took five minutes to walk from one house to the other. Two if you cycled.

Turning into the main street, which led out onto the moors, they passed the handful of buildings that made up Endrith village: a butcher's shop, a mini market, a newsagent, and a curiosity shop that sold everything from nails and wallpaper paste to antiques. Further along was the playground where most of the village kids hung out – even the older ones – and a chapel. Saint Andrew and All the Saints' Chapel was ancient, made from big blocks of dark grey granite, with a cracked bell and a weathercock that creaked like a rusty gate whenever the wind changed direction.

Leaving the village behind, they turned onto a

narrow, puddle-spattered lane. It was edged by a low drystone wall that did nothing to stop the sheep from wandering into the road. Jack's dad manoeuvred carefully around a startled-looking ewe, its thin legs looking overburdened beneath its huge fleece.

To their left, Endrith Mountain towered majestically over the landscape, its peak capped with grey cloud, while to the right stretched the moors, the brilliant orange bracken shrouded now in an eerie morning mist that lay like a soft, white blanket.

They motored on, passing overgrown tracks that wound their way down into the valley, past the sprawling Endrith Forest where Jack had once spotted a whole family of deer. But then the landscape changed – the greenery stopped abruptly and in its place appeared a mess of dark orange clay and mounds of earth. They looked ugly and out of place amongst the natural colours of the Highlands. The green topsoil had been stripped away, first by giant bulldozers, and then, more gently, by people with trowels.

There were no construction workers now, but there was plenty of evidence that they would soon be returning. Heavy digging machinery stood idle, piles of huge concrete pipes were waiting to be laid under the new road, and a massive reel of cable stood on end, looking like it might roll down the hill into the field below at any moment.

"Looks more like a bulldozer cemetery than a dig," murmured Jack, as his dad parked close to the fenced-off excavation site.

"Get your wellies on, lads," said the professor, hauling a bag of equipment from his car. "I'll go and find someone who can show you the ropes."

Eagerly, Jack and Cameron swapped their trainers for wellingtons. Then they stood with fingers looped through the wire fencing, gazing in awe down into the crater.

"Oh, wow!" Jack gasped, his breath hanging like a cloud in the chill morning air. A huge square had been carved out of the earth. It was over a metre deep, with steps cut into the muddy side walls and reinforced with planks, so that people could climb in and out easily. Even though it was early, there were at least a dozen figures moving around the crater in the cold morning mist.

And there, lying just as they had fallen thousands of years ago, were the bones of a giant woolly mammoth. The skeleton was blackened but the boys could still make out the shape of its legs. As they walked round the crater, they could see the outline of its whole body.

"Look at the angle of its front leg," breathed Jack. "It's raised really high, as if it was charging along, and the back leg's pushed straight out behind it. You can see how powerful and strong it must have been. Just think, Cameron, it must have come thundering along here...I wonder why it was running?"

"Rampaging," said Cameron. "That's what elephants do. And a mammoth is from the elephant family, isn't it? They go on the rampage – when they're afraid, or angry, or mad. I suppose something must have made it angry, or scared."

"Can't imagine anything scaring something *that* big," murmured Jack, wrinkling his nose as he caught a strange smell. It wasn't the smell of wet earth or clay, it was something else...

"Well whatever was chasing it must have caught and killed it," stated Cameron, staring mesmerized.

"Maybe it was a hunter – a prehistoric caveman hunter," suggested Jack, noticing how small all the workers looked against the mammoth's skeleton – insignificant almost.

"Or the beast," suggested Cameron with a glint in his eye. "Maybe the beast was chasing it. It could have been alive around the same time as the mammoth."

Jack groaned. "Cam, there's no proof that sabre-toothed tigers ever lived in Scotland. And even if they did, there's definitely no proof that the ghost of one is still hanging around – apart from two kids saying they saw it and it chased them. Hardly cast-iron evidence! So *please* stop going on about your beast!"

"You'd have said woolly mammoths didn't exist in Scotland till a few weeks ago," remarked Cameron smugly.

"Okay, so when they find a sabre-toothed tiger's skeleton I might start thinking differently – until then, it's rubbish!"

Jack's dad came striding back, interrupting their discussion. "Okay, lads! That's all sorted."

"Excellent!" exclaimed Jack.

"Thank you, Mr. MacDonald, we won't mess around," promised Cameron.

"I'm sure you won't," smiled the professor. "So, lads, what you'll be doing is working on that bottom left-hand corner – to be precise, the mammoth's back foot. Sally down there will show you what to do, but basically you'll be cleaning up bones and putting them into plastic bags ready for Sally to label and index. All set?"

"Aye, of course!" beamed Jack, eager to get closer to that prehistoric skeleton.

"Don't slip!" warned his dad, leading the way through the gate and along the perimeter of the crater to the nearest set of steps.

Jack and Cameron followed, doing their best not to skid in the mud. Getting closer to the mammoth's darkened bones, the strange smell seemed stronger to Jack. It wasn't decay exactly, but definitely a raw, animal-like odour.

"I can smell it," Jack murmured, feeling suddenly shaky now that he was so close to something so ancient.

"Smell what?" asked Cameron.

Climbing down the makeshift steps, into the mammoth's grave, Jack said quietly, "I can smell the mammoth."

Standing inside the excavated hollow, the mass of ancient grey-black, mud-smothered bones stretched out before them and, for a second, Jack wished he was anywhere other than here, in a huge smelly grave, standing next to the corpse of a prehistoric monster.

But Cameron looked elated.

Jack's dad introduced them to Sally. She was a palaeontology student who had come all the way from Wales to work on this dig. She was about nineteen, with mud on her cheeks and her blonde hair tied back in a ponytail.

"Hello there!" She smiled, moving to shake hands, then changing her mind. "Whoops, sorry guys, I'm a bit muddy – although you'll be in exactly the same state in a few minutes."

She cheerfully explained what they had to do, providing them with trays and little brushes, and a pile of plastic bags, labels and marker pens.

Cameron was keen to get started, but Jack hesitated. He stared at a small knobbly bone and suddenly a wave of nausea washed over him. This wasn't a piece of ancient pottery or a caveman's prehistoric axe. This was a bone from a dead animal.

Sally was watching Jack with a bemused smile on her face. "Well, go on then! It won't bite you!"

But still Jack hesitated. He suddenly realized that he didn't want to take this creature apart, bone by bone. Suddenly he understood his mum's sentiments, and her words echoed through his head...

It's a shame it can't be left in peace...

But Cameron was already on his knees, brushing mud from a bone. He glanced up, his eyes sparkling excitedly. "Look at this, Jack, a woolly mammoth's big toe!"

Jack realized he really had no choice. Coming here was his idea after all. He could hardly back out now. So, very warily, he kneeled down and picked up a blackened bone. Carefully, he began to brush away the mud. "*Sorry*," he murmured, under his breath.

They worked all morning, with the trays of plastic bags gradually mounting up, although it didn't get any easier for Jack. He still felt squeamish at handling bones. Cameron, however, didn't seem to mind at all, and Sally was clearly loving every second of it. She chatted away non-stop, regaling them with tales from other digs she'd been on and the exciting things she'd unearthed.

Around midday, as everyone was starting to get hungry, Jack glanced up and spotted his dad and another palaeontologist struggling to lift a huge bone.

"We're making good progress, boys..." remarked Sally. Then she followed Jack's gaze. "Oh wow! Just look at that! Your dad's excavating the mammoth's breastbone. That's where its heart would have been..."

The words had barely left her mouth when a sudden violent shudder vibrated from one end of the crater to the other.

Everyone instantly stopped what they were doing and looked anxiously at one another, as if for confirmation that they weren't imagining the shaking and trembling of the ground beneath them.

The vibrations continued, making puddles ripple and splash, and a second later a thunderous rumble rolled across the valley.

"What's happening?" Jack gasped, aware that the horrible stench had grown worse.

The juddering, trembling sensation shuddered on. Everyone quickly got to their feet. Cameron grabbed hold of Jack's arm as the earth shook crazily.

The side walls of the crater began to crumble. Mud started to slide down them, slithering over the unearthed bones, swamping people's feet.

Jack felt his boots starting to stick fast in the rising tide of mud and clay just as his dad shouted, "Earthquake! Everyone out of the crater – quickly!"

It was impossible to move quickly with feet weighed down in sludge, and everyone struggled to wade through the sea of moving wet clay.

"My feet are stuck!" Cameron cried, still clinging on to Jack's arm.

Yanking his own feet from the claggy mess that was already up to his ankles, Jack yelled, "Pull, Cam! Keep your feet moving!"

Skidding and squelching, they staggered to the nearest steps, only to find that the wooden planks had become dislodged in the mudslide. Panic flared in Cameron's eyes for a second, but a moment later Jack's dad was beside them.

"Don't panic, lads," he said reassuringly, hauling himself out of the crater, then reaching down to pull Jack, Cameron, Sally and half-a-dozen others out too.

And all the while the earth vibrated and the trembling echo rumbled on and on – like thunder that wouldn't roll away.

Then, as suddenly as it had started, the tremor stopped.

No one spoke. Everyone stood motionless,

stunned and unnaturally silent as the growl of thunder droned away into the distance. The ground ceased its trembling. The sliding mud settled.

Still no one said a word and an eerie silence hung over the excavation site until, finally, Jack's dad called out, "Is everyone okay?"

A hubbub of chatter erupted. Everyone began talking at once, exclaiming shock and surprise. It was then that Jack noticed the horrible stench had gone.

chapter three

High on the mountainous ridge, yellow slitted eyes blinked open. A massive paw twitched, sending a pebble skittering over the edge, to bounce all the way to the valley below.

Stretching out mighty limbs, Karbel extended the black talons that in life could have ripped almost any living creature to shreds, and glared out over the valley where he had slumbered for thousands of years. He did not care to be awoken so abruptly from his eternal sleep.

His sharp, alert eyes suddenly narrowed and darkened.

He sensed it instantly. There was a new presence in his domain.

He rose to his feet, a low warning growl rumbling from his throat. Yet anyone looking could not have spotted the formidable prehistoric beast standing proud and fearsome, high on a mountain ridge, its vicious sabre-teeth bared. They would have seen only the desolation of a Highland mountainside on a cold winter's afternoon.

Yet Karbel was there all the same. The spirit of a beast that had prowled this earth ten thousand years ago. A spirit that was alert and powerful.

A ghostly creature that was aware, suddenly, that in this spirit world of his, he – Karbel – was no longer alone.

Another spirit had entered his world – and it was evil.

* * *

No one was in a hurry to go back into the excavation crater. Instead they all headed towards the mobile snack bar for coffees and teas. Jack's dad steered the boys out through the wire fence. "Well, that's something you don't experience every day! Are you both okay? Not too shaken up?"

Jack felt a bit wobbly and Cameron had turned as white as a ghost. The sensation of sinking ankle-deep in mud had been horrible. It was like being on the beach with the tide coming in. Only this wasn't nice hot sand, this was stinking claggy mud and ancient old bones.

"I thought we were supposed to dig up the mammoth's bones," muttered Cameron unhappily. "Not get buried with them!"

Jack suddenly felt quite sick again.

Although he didn't say so, Jack was secretly pleased when his dad told him and Cameron that they wouldn't be allowed back on the excavation site that day – in case another tremor occurred.

"Hose your boots off, lads, and get into your trainers," the professor instructed after they'd had a cup of tea and a hot pasty from the mobile food van. "You'll have to amuse yourselves for a while. I've got to put a few more hours in here. That tremor has set us right back."

"An earthquake like that can't be normal, can it, Mr. MacDonald?" said Cameron, still shaking slightly as they headed back to the car.

"It's very unusual," he agreed. "I'll be ringing around to see what I can find out. But in the meantime, I'd prefer it if you lads took yourselves off away from all this mud and rubble, just until we find out what caused the tremor."

Getting their shoes from the car boot, Jack spotted his football. "We'll be okay, Dad. We'll have a bit of a kick-about."

"Good idea." The professor smiled. "There's that nice stretch of pasture just over the hill, down towards the stream. Make sure you get back here before it gets dark and we'll head off home then."

"Aye, okay," said Jack, tucking his football under his arm. He and Cameron knew the pasture and stream well. The stream was alive with wildlife and was a favourite fishing and bird-watching spot. There was a bird hide where you could sit and watch the wildlife through binoculars. Jack had seen kingfishers, crossbills and corncrakes – even an osprey one summer.

"See you later then, Dad," Jack said cheerfully, as he and Cameron set off along the half-constructed roadway, dribbling the ball between them.

"That was pretty weird, wasn't it?" Cameron remarked as they headed away from the excavation site.

"You're not joking!" agreed Jack, passing the ball back to his mate with a neat little back kick. "Earthquakes, mammoths...it's totally mad!"

Mounds of soil were piled up along the way and massive earth-moving vehicles stood abandoned, as if they, like the mammoth, had suddenly been stopped dead in their tracks.

Nothing moved. Everything was silent and still, and Jack's brief cheerful mood began to ebb away. With all the heavy machinery standing idle, work half finished, and not a living soul in sight, it felt like a ghost town.

"It would be good if they actually did dig up the bones of a sabre-toothed tiger, wouldn't it?" Cameron mused, kicking the ball and sending it skittering along the half-made road to bounce off a pyramid of massive concrete pipes.

"Y'know what, Cam? If that tiger really did exist, you'd run a mile!" Jack teased.

"But ghosts do exist," Cameron stated. "My gran heard the actual sounds of the Battle of Endrith on the morning of its anniversary, when she was young. And when she died, last year, I saw her ghost in her garden when Mum and I were sorting out all her stuff – I did tell you at the time. The only reason you don't want to believe is because *you've* never seen a ghost!"

"I deal in facts. Cold, hard facts and concrete evidence," Jack retorted, sounding very much like his dad. Although, deep down inside, he couldn't help thinking that the eerie silence around them did feel a bit spooky.

Reaching the pyramid of concrete pipes that

were stacked up high, Cameron stretched up on his tiptoes to peer into one of them. "You could have a great game of hide-and-seek round here. These pipes are big enough to climb into."

"I know... Hey, Cam, did you smell that odd smell when we were at the excavation site? Like an animal smell, only horrible and decaying?"

Cameron shrugged. "No. I heard you mutter something about a smell back at the dig – what were you on about? I didn't smell anything."

"It was a right stink! You must have smelled it!"

"No. All I could smell was clay."

Jack felt his stomach tighten at the memory of the stench. "It wasn't clay. I know what clay smells like. This was a really nasty, vile stink."

Cameron gave another shrug. "Well, I didn't smell anything unusual. I have got a bit of a cold, though."

Jack shook his head, wondering how anyone could have failed to notice it. He gave the ball a powerful kick. "Come on, Cam, let's head over to the stream. I've seen enough mud for one day."

Cameron ran after the ball, and between them they dribbled it around the mounds of earth and machinery to where the ground was grassy again and the air was fresh and clean. Then they jogged along, passing the ball to each other, kicking it harder and further every time.

They knew this area well. Ever since they'd been allowed to play beyond the village, they would often ride their bikes down to the stream, or cycle through the forest to Endrith Valley and spend the day there – fishing, rock climbing, exploring caves...or, more recently, taking part in Cameron's favourite sport – beast hunting – looking for signs of the mythical sabre-toothed tiger around the caves in the mountainside.

"Just think," said Cameron, as he drop-kicked the ball back to Jack, "woolly mammoths have actually roamed around right here. Imagine those huge, lumbering animals trundling along, with their long, matted coats and those massive, curved tusks."

Jack preferred to imagine them that way, rather than rotting in a hole in the ground, but he couldn't get the image of the skeleton out of his head, and the thought of handling those bones still made him shudder. In an effort to rid himself of the memory, he booted the ball as hard as he could.

It sailed over Cameron's head and disappeared down a slope.

"Cheers, pal!" called Cameron as he went racing after it, skidding and sliding down the grass, all the way to the bottom.

It was a long while before he reappeared. "Kick it back, then!" shouted Jack.

"I would if I could find it!" Cameron yelled from the bottom of the slope.

Jack wandered over and stood watching his friend rooting around in the long grass below him.

"That's odd, it's vanished," Cameron complained. "Where's it gone then?"

"Pretty powerful kick, don't you think?" Jack boasted, slithering down the slope to help look for the ball.

The smell hit him instantly. An earthy, animal smell, like something from a farmyard, only stronger – a rotting, decomposed stench. His stomach churned. "There it is again."

"There what is?"

"The smell!"

"What smell? I can't smell anything," Cameron muttered, still rooting around in the long grass.

"You need to get your sinuses sorted," Jack exclaimed, trying not to breathe too deeply. He spotted something then...something red and white, and flattened into the ground. Slowly, he stooped to pick it up. It was his football, as flat as a pancake. Burst at the seams and totally deflated.

Miserably, Jack dangled it from his fingertips. "Some kick!" he wailed.

"It looks like it's been run over by a steamroller!" said Cameron, staring in disbelief at the crushed football. Then, looking at Jack, he added, "They'll be wanting to sign you up for Celtic!"

"How did it get so flat?" Jack puzzled, examining his football and the undergrowth to see what it had landed on. "I can't see anything sharp."

Cameron looked vaguely impressed. "Maybe you just don't know your own strength."

"Hah!" Jack raised his eyebrows. "So now what?"

Cameron shrugged. "We could head on down to the stream and do a bit of birdwatching from the hide."

"Yeah, may as well," agreed Jack, glad that the smell seemed to be fading now.

Cameron took the squashed ball from Jack as they headed off towards the banks of the stream in the distance. "It looks like something really heavy has slammed down on it... You know, I thought I heard this popping noise when I was rooting about for it..." His voice trailed away.

"What?" Jack asked, glancing curiously at him.

"I heard a popping noise after it had landed down there," Cameron stated. "*After!*"

"And your point is?"

"Well, if it landed on something sharp that punctured it, it would have popped *as* it landed, wouldn't it? Not a minute or so later."

Jack pulled a face. "Well, all I know is that I'm going to need a new football."

With Cameron still puzzling over how the ball could have deflated so quickly, they wandered across the open pasture. It was a big expanse of grassy moorland, great for playing football – if you had one. In the centre stood one solitary oak tree, or rather the remains of an oak tree. At some time in the past it must have been struck by lightning, because now its skeletal branches were twisted and bleached almost white.

As a complete contrast, Endrith Forest rose up to their left – a mass of tall, straight pines and beautiful silver-birch trees. It was a forest that was alive with wildlife. Jack had seen deer – even a stag once – and foxes and rabbits. And when he'd been here at dusk with his dad after fishing trips, they'd seen thousands and thousands of starlings swarming back to roost.

"We should have brought our bikes," remarked Cameron, glancing back over the distance they'd already walked.

"Yes, well, we thought we were going to be

excavating all day, not mooching around... Hey, look!" he exclaimed, as something above them caught his eye. "That bird – it's a golden eagle, isn't it? Oh wow!"

They both stopped to stare upwards, where a bird with a huge wingspan was soaring high amongst the clouds.

"You could be right," agreed Cameron. "There's usually some binoculars in the bird hide – we might be able to get a good look at it if we're quick."

They increased their pace as they headed towards the stream. The bird hide was a great place to hang out and watch the wildlife without being seen. It wasn't much more than a shed, camouflaged on the outside by a mesh of sticks and twigs woven together. Inside it was quite comfortable, with chairs and slits in the walls where you could peep out.

They walked on, chatting about golden eagles, and the osprey that Jack had spotted the summer before last, but then Jack frowned. Something wasn't right...

Something was different...

"I'd love to see a white-tailed eagle," Cameron was saying. "A kid at school reckoned he saw one flying around Endrith Mountain last Christmas..."

"Something's missing!"

"What?"

Jack stopped dead. "Something's missing."

"What are you on about?" Cameron asked, pushing his spectacles to the top of his nose. "All looks pretty normal to me."

"The bird hide!" Jack exclaimed, staring towards the loch. "It's gone!"

"What? No way!" Then Cameron's mouth dropped. "You're right, it's not there!"

They sprinted across the grass to where the bird hide had stood on the edge of the stream. As they grew nearer, they saw a fragmented pile of wood littering the ground.

"No!" Jack gasped, staggering to a halt to stare in horror at the bird hide. It had been smashed to smithereens. "What lunatic's done this?"

"Who'd be so mean...?" Cameron murmured

in disbelief, shifting the pile of rubble with his foot. He bent down and pulled a pair of binoculars from the debris. "Vandals would have taken these, wouldn't they?"

"You'd think so," murmured Jack, feeling sick at the sight of the wreckage. "But you'd have to be insane to do this!"

"Someone's gone at it with a sledgehammer!" Cameron said angrily.

Numbed and sickened by the mindless destruction, Jack felt his throat constrict. He swallowed hard, his stomach churning as he stared in dismay at the smashed hide.

Then he realized what was really making him feel so ill.

The smell was back.

chapter four

As Karbel looked out over the Valley of Shadows, his senses were alert once more. Death had not taken away his basic instincts. His sharp yellow eyes were as watchful as ever, his hearing attuned to the smallest sound, his sense of smell keener in death than in life.

But he needed none of his heightened senses to recognize the monstrous invasion of his valley.

The stench of decay hung like a dead weight in the air. It was the stench of evil, and it had no place in Karbel's world.

Deep within his breast he felt his anger rise and, throwing back his mighty head, he bellowed out a roar that in life would have instilled terror in all who heard it.

But his roar now was silent. It drifted across the valley as soft as a whisper – yet still a flock of starlings took flight from the distant forest and swarmed into the sky, like a shifting black cloud, alarmed by the unknown disturbance on the wind.

Karbel's intense gaze scanned the valley below him. Unhindered by mortal sight, he looked across the grey waters of the loch to the woody depths of the forest. He had slumbered here on Endrith Mountain for thousands of years. And in his waking moments he had watched seasons come and go; he had endured humans with their irritating and dangerous ways; he had observed the spirits of raging warriors returning, time after time, to repeat their senseless slaying of each other...

But this evil presence which had awoken him now was by far the greatest disturbance Karbel had ever felt. It had dared enter his spiritual plane – invaded the space in which he dwelled alone, suspended between life and death.

Karbel's restless movements were creating turmoil. Pebbles and stones beneath his feet shot in all directions. He began to feel his heart pump blood through his veins once more. And now a strange shimmering light began to take form on that rocky ledge, barely visible had anyone glanced that way. It was a glow that shifted back and forth, high on the desolate mountainside.

Anger, pain, anguish, the desire to hunt and kill – any of these emotions could trigger Karbel's manifestations – his return to physical form with all the power and strength he possessed when alive.

Although manifestations were brief – and rare – they left him exhausted. The process was not an easy one. He needed time for his energies to build up before manifestation occurred. Basic desires fuelled his determination, transforming their energy – allowing him to become truly alive once more, even if only for a moment. There had been times over the centuries when Karbel could not fend off those basic urges and emotions. They had not died when his mortal body had succumbed to the blade of a boy's knife so many millennia ago.

Suddenly his mind filled with memories of a brief awakening, just two summers ago. Karbel uttered a low, dangerous growl at the thought...

At that time, a boy had come to the valley. This boy resembled the young male who had stabbed Karbel through the heart all those thousands of years before. He acted with the same bravery. Karbel had believed it was indeed the same boy, returned to rob him of his very soul.

Two summers ago, Karbel's rage had caused him to manifest himself and hunt the boy down...

But his most recent manifestation had been just one summer ago, when a cub had briefly appeared in the valley to tug at his heart strings, reminding him of his own siblings and his mother. Karbel had desperately desired the cub as a companion to ease his lonely existence.

But it was not to be.

Now, suddenly, the pain of his endless solitude, coupled with his rage over the unwelcome presence of evil, ravaged him once more. Karbel threw back his great head and let out an agonizing roar that was carried off with the wind.

But the sound reached the very edge of hearing. No human ears could distinguish it, yet the more sensitive small forest creatures cringed with fear from its intensity.

Karbel sensed their distress now, as his awakened presence created confusion and alarm throughout the valley and forest.

And the creatures were right to be afraid...

Returning miserably to the excavation site, Jack told his dad about the destroyed bird hide. Dismayed, the professor put in a phone call to the local police station, then got back to his excavation work. Jack and Cameron hung about watching another television film crew making a news report.

At dinner that night, Jack and his parents sat round discussing what a weird day it had been.

"What puzzles me most," said Jack's dad, "is the fact that the earth tremor didn't register anywhere. I've phoned the meteorological office, the town hall, even the police, and nothing was heard or felt anywhere else apart from by us, in the crater."

"And we *definitely* all felt it!" Jack exclaimed. "And smelled it. Dad, did you smell that really vile smell when it was all going on?"

"I did actually, son. Haven't a clue what that was – some sort of trapped gas escaping from underground, I suppose."

Jack's mum looked puzzled. "Could there just have been a very small localized tremor for some reason?"

Professor MacDonald rubbed his chin. "I can't think why, unless the construction work has caused some subsidence – which is worrying. It needs to be investigated if those roadworks are to continue. You wouldn't want the ground shaking or collapsing like that when there's traffic going along it."

"Maybe the tremor destroyed the bird hide," Jack suggested. "Perhaps all that shaking made it fall down. It wasn't very sturdy, was it?"

His dad considered the possibility for a second. "Well, maybe – although that would mean the tremor travelled quite some distance. In which case, it should have registered *somewhere*."

They lapsed into silence as they got on with their dinner, then Jack remembered something else.

"Oh, and there was another disaster!"

"Now what?" both his parents exclaimed anxiously.

"My football burst today. It went as flat as a pancake."

"Is that all?" His mum sighed with relief. "I'm sure we can get you another one. Now eat up, we've apple pie for afters."

* * *

The ringing of a cracked church bell woke Jack the next morning, reminding him that it was Sunday. He peered out of the window to see a bright, clear, frosty morning. A perfect day for a bike ride with Cameron.

"So what did the tremor measure on the Richter scale?" Cameron was eager to know, when Jack called round for him after breakfast.

"You won't believe this," said Jack, as they set off towards the outskirts of the village. "It didn't register at all. Not on the Richter scale, not anywhere!"

"You're joking!"

"No! Only the people at the dig felt it."

"Weird! Although Mum and Dad didn't feel anything either," Cameron said as they cycled past the park, where a handful of kids were playing on the swings and slides, then down the lane, with its crumbling mossy wall. As usual, a few stray sheep were wandering all over the road. They broke into a cumbersome trot as Jack and Cameron approached.

"Is your dad going back to the site today?"

"Aye! He was just getting ready when I came out," said Jack. "Let's hope nothing else weird happens today. It could really set them back."

They cycled on, turning onto an uphill zigzagging track, which led eventually to Endrith Forest. The track was rarely used and gorse and ferns crowded in on all sides. They pedalled on until they reached the brow of the hill, where the landscape stretched out in a vast panorama of moorland, fields and forest – and a handful of people crowded around something sprawled out in a field.

"Now what!" Jack uttered, feeling suddenly cold.

"What is it?" Cameron murmured. "Is that...? It looks like a hairy coo...is it dead? It's covered in blood! Come on!" He shot off along the track.

Reluctantly, Jack followed. He didn't want to see a dead Highland cow, especially not one covered in blood. Hairy coos, as the locals liked to call them, were big, beautiful beasts with long, golden, raggedy coats and massive curved horns. They were friendly too, despite their size.

There was a policeman amongst the small crowd of farmhands. He spotted the boys pedalling towards him and called to them. "A word, please, lads," he said, raising a hand.

"What's happened? Is it dead?" Cameron asked breathlessly, as he skidded to a halt.

Jack pulled up alongside him and glanced briefly at the animal, before turning away. There was an ugly bleeding wound down its side and the poor thing was lying there wide-eyed.

"The vet's doing what he can," said the police officer. "Were you lads around earlier? Did you see anything?"

"No," murmured Jack, feeling sorry for the creature. "We haven't been along here in ages. What's happened to it?"

The officer scratched his head, but one of the farmhands interrupted. "Well, I'd say it's been fighting with another of the herd. Something long and sharp – a horn, like as not – has ripped it right open. It actually looks as if it's been tossed in the air to land here."

"How do you know?" asked Cameron,

craning his neck to get a better look.

The farmhand pointed to the rest of the herd on the far side of a drystone wall. "Because it ought to be in *that* field!"

"You're joking!" Cameron gasped.

Jack stared in total disbelief. "But these are placid animals – they don't fight!"

"Well something's obviously upset them. I can't understand why they'd turn on one another, though." The farmhand shook his head. "These cattle weigh nearly a tonne – I can't imagine how another of the herd could have tossed it over a wall."

"If you hear of anyone who witnessed anything, be sure to let me know," the police officer said.

"Aye, we will," said Cameron, getting ready to cycle off. Then he hesitated and asked, "Are you going to investigate the bird hide as well? Someone's smashed it to bits."

"That's where I was headed when I got this call," said the officer. "I'll take a look when I've finished here." He rubbed his chin. "Unusual goings-on for this part of the world."

A tingle of unease ran down Jack's spine. "You don't think there's some maniac running around, do you? Smashing things up and trying to kill the cattle?"

"I really don't think so, son. And I shouldn't worry too much about it!" The officer smiled kindly. "Go on, you lads had best be on your way."

With a last glance back at the injured animal, Jack and Cameron cycled on towards the forest. Jack's head was spinning with all the strange things that had happened.

"This is all so weird." He frowned, as the massive forest trees loomed up ahead. "What's going on? First an earthquake, except we were the only ones that felt it, then the bird hide gets flattened. And now the cattle are turning on each other."

Cameron looked steadily at Jack. "You've forgotten something."

"Have I...? What's that?"

"Your football getting splattered."

Jack managed a feeble smile. "That's hardly in

the same league as a huge hairy coo being speared and chucked over a wall."

"But it's still a mystery," Cameron insisted, as they both dismounted to push their bikes over some rough terrain. "Footballs don't deflate that quickly, unless something's forced all the air out."

Jack sighed. "Well, it beats me. If I think of an explanation, Cam, I'll let you know."

For a second, Cameron seemed about to suggest something. Then, as if thinking better of it, he snapped his mouth shut and walked on, pushing his bike into the shadowy forest.

A canopy of greenery blocked out the wintery sunlight, while underfoot a deep layer of fallen leaves cushioned their step. They walked deeper into the forest, lost in conversation about the bird hide and the earthquake and the cow. Thoughts of the mammoth's skeleton, that had occupied Jack's mind so intensely a few days ago, now seemed almost insignificant.

The ground was still damp from the recent rain and they had to stop frequently to unclog dead leaves from their bike wheels, as they strolled along the forest pathway that led through to Endrith Valley.

"Let's hope nothing weird has happened in the valley," Jack said, disentangling some twigs from his wheel spokes.

"Like what? There are no bird hides to flatten, no hairy coos around here..." Cameron's eyes sparkled behind his spectacles. "Unless the bones of the beast have suddenly unearthed themselves."

"You're obsessed with that beast rumour!" Jack exclaimed. His voice sounded loud in the still air and he was aware, suddenly, of how quiet the forest was today. Usually you'd hear the birds singing and the squeaks and chirps of little animals and insects. But today it was silent... unnaturally silent.

"I had a thought actually..." Cameron began. Then he stared at Jack. "What's up?"

Jack glanced back over his shoulder. The silence was unnerving. "Nothing, it's just a bit quiet, don't you reckon?"

"It's always quiet. Anyway, what I was

thinking..." He hesitated again. "You'll say I'm daft..."

Jack attempted to concentrate on Cameron's words and not let the deadly silence of the forest get to him. "Go on then, what's this nutty idea you've come up with?"

Cameron took a deep breath. "Well, if the valley *is* haunted, like they say, maybe the ghost of the beast or the ghosts of those ancient warriors came to investigate the mammoth's skeleton being dug up. Maybe it wasn't an earthquake after all, but their spooky presence that we felt shaking the ground. And maybe all the other weird things are down to them too." He looked at Jack. "Go on, say it – I'm mad."

Under different circumstances, Jack would definitely have told his friend he'd got a screw loose, only right now these weird things that had been happening were a real mystery. Not even his dad had a convincing answer for the earth tremor. Okay, the flattened bird hide *had* to be vandals. And maybe his squashed football was just a bit of bad luck – it must have come down hard on something sharp. But the cow...

"Say something then!" Cameron demanded, staring at Jack, as they pushed their bikes along. "It's not such a stupid idea, is it?"

"So what are you suggesting, exactly?" Jack sighed, still unwilling to believe that excavating a prehistoric creature's remains could have triggered something supernatural. Yet he was puzzled by the unnatural feeling about the forest today. Nothing moved. Nothing scampered underfoot. No squirrels or rabbits, not even a bird fluttered through the overhead branches.

It didn't seem to bother Cameron, though – he was busy elaborating on his latest theory. "It sounds barmy, but what if it wasn't a cattle fight that injured the coo? What if it was the sabre teeth of the beast? Remember those kids who said they'd been stalked by the ghost of a sabre-toothed tiger, down in the Valley? They said it clawed the boy's shirt. They said it manifested itself – that it became real! Maybe it's happening again. Maybe it's come back to life and isn't happy. Maybe it smashed the bird hide, too!"

Jack really wished his friend would stop going on about ghosts and dead animals coming back to life. He felt uneasy and jittery enough. He'd never known the forest to be so silent. It was as if all the wildlife had left, or were hiding and holding their breath.

As if they sensed something was going to happen.

The jittery sensation in his stomach warned Jack that things definitely weren't right, but he did his best to ignore it and concentrate on Cameron's ideas. Deliberately, he scoffed at the thought of ghosts coming back to haunt them. "Imagination overload, Cam! You'll be saying it was the beast that punctured my football next."

"Maybe it did!" Cameron went on excitedly. "Those kids actually saw the beast. It was all in the newspaper. So why shouldn't it still be around?"

"Exactly – it was in the paper! It was a story to sell newspapers. They made it up or imagined it," stated Jack. "At least loads of people have heard the sound of warriors battling over the years, not just a couple of kids. That's slightly more believable than sabre-toothed tigers." Flippantly, he added, "Hey, maybe the warriors were re-enacting the Battle of Endrith and the hairy coo got in the way."

Cameron considered the idea, then shook his head. "No, it couldn't have been that. Battle sounds have only been heard on the anniversary of the battle, which is in August, I think."

"Cam, if what you're suggesting is right, do you realize the danger we'd all be in? If there really was a vicious ghost of a sabre-toothed tiger on the prowl, that could inflict horrible wounds on whatever or whoever it felt like attacking, we'd all be in terrible danger. *All* of us!"

Cameron's eyes widened. "Aye! Scary that, isn't it?"

"*Very* scary!" agreed Jack, dragging another clump of damp leaves from his bicycle spokes. "So it's a good job ghosts *don't* exist..."

A noise behind them made them jump. After the intense silence, the cracking sound was like a gunshot.

"What's that?" Cameron asked sharply, looking back.

"Sounded like a branch snapping."

"Why?" Cameron asked, puzzled. "Why would a branch snap just like that?"

"I don't know..."

A moment later they heard another crack. It was definitely coming from behind them, back the way they'd come. And it was definitely the sound of breaking wood. Not little twigs either, but loud snaps and crunches, like huge branches being broken clean off.

A third sharp crack echoed through the forest, and then another, louder than before...and closer. The noise continued, now rolling towards them – harsh cracking sounds, one after the other, followed by the crash of wood splintering as it hit the ground, getting louder and faster all the time.

Soon it was one long, crazy, chaotic noise, as if a silent bulldozer was running amok, smashing through the trees.

The boys stood, riveted to the spot, staring back through the forest to where the noise was coming from. Then Jack spotted movement through a stand of pine trees.

"There!" he breathed, pointing. "I saw a branch falling! Look, there's another."

"Why?" Cameron whispered. "Why are branches falling off the trees like that? Branches don't just fall off trees. It's crazy!"

"There're not *falling* off the trees," Jack replied, as he stared in horror at the path of destruction heading their way. "They're being ripped off!"

The more they stared, the more it became obvious that there was a pattern to this chaos. The trees were being vandalized in a straight line... A line heading directly towards them.

As another branch crashed down, vibrations shuddered through the ground. Then, seconds later, a tall silver-birch tree simply toppled over, snapping smaller saplings as it fell to the ground with an almighty creaking, groaning sound, followed by a tremendous thud that shook the earth beneath the boys' feet.

"Jack, the forest's caving in!" Cameron cried,

scrambling frantically back onto his bike to escape.

Jack couldn't move. His feet were riveted to the ground as the forest disintegrated before his eyes, leaving a gaping pathway of broken trees and crushed woodland. *Something* was moving towards them, flattening everything in its way.

"We're in its path!" Cameron yelled, throwing down his bike. Its wheels were clogged with leaves and refused to turn. "Something's coming right at us. Run, Jack, run!"

Vibrations thundered through the ground.

"Earthquake?" Jack gasped, staring in blind terror as tree after tree fell or was smashed sideways by some invisible, unstoppable force.

Beneath their feet they felt strange tremors, like heavy piledrivers pounding into the ground, *thud...thud...thud...thud...* It seemed like something massive was running – *rampaging* – through the forest!

Instantly, instinctively, Jack knew what it was. But that was impossible... It couldn't be. His mum's words echoed through his brain.

It's a shame it can't be left in peace...

Another birch tree lurched violently to one side. Its muddy roots shot up out of the ground. And then a mighty pine fell in the opposite direction, groaning horrendously as its soil-covered roots were levered up out of the earth.

Thud...thud...thud...thud... It was coming closer all the time.

Massive feet slammed into the ground.

Now Jack understood why his football had popped, and why the bird hide had been reduced to matchwood, and why the poor cow had been savaged – the creature must have tried to stand up to the terrible danger that had thundered its way.

Too stunned to move, Jack stared in disbelief at the gaping corridor of broken trees. It was almost here, almost upon them, but although his eyes searched frantically to catch a glimpse of this rampant monster, he could see nothing, nothing at all.

In such a state of shock, he didn't realize that Cameron was screaming in his ear to run and dragging on his arm like crazy.

"Run!" Cameron's voice finally got through to him, and Jack felt himself being yanked fiercely to one side, to land, with Cameron, in a tangled heap on the ground. A second later, a massive blast of ice-cold energy swept past them, as if they had been standing too close to a road when a juggernaut had sped by. And with the icy rush came a stench of rot and decay so vile that Jack collapsed, retching, into the long grass.

He looked back up to see their abandoned bikes suddenly mangled before his eyes, as if a giant invisible sledgehammer had slammed viciously down onto their frames, turning them instantly into junk.

Trembling with shock, the boys watched the rampage continue, tree branches crumbling like matchwood, as the invisible force crashed blindly through the undergrowth, heading straight towards Endrith Valley.

The rotting stench faded.

The boys were a long time moving. For an age, they cowered behind a fallen tree trunk, watching the trail of destruction head further into the distance. Only when the earth had ceased to shudder and vibrate, and the last hint of the stench had gone, did they scramble to their feet...and run.

chapter five

From his mountain vantage point, Karbel had watched and listened throughout the night. He had raised his head into the wind, smelling the air, waiting for the unwelcome, evil presence to show itself. Now, in the morning light, the stench grew stronger and the noise of destruction began to reach him.

He watched, hissing and spitting, while the

canopy of trees far below swayed as something blundered through them. But even Karbel could not yet identify the invisible monster.

As tree after tree crashed to the ground, Karbel's black gums drew back to reveal two vicious sabre teeth, and his seething snarl drifted out onto the wind.

Whatever this monstrous evil was that dared to disturb his peaceful existence, it had almost reached the forest boundary. Soon it would emerge into his valley.

And he would be waiting...

Opening wide his massive sabre jaws, Karbel roared out a defiant warning to the approaching menace, and a flock of waterfowl nestling in the reeds on the loch shores far below suddenly flew, startled, into the air.

Karbel sprang, bounding from ridge to ridge, zigzagging down the mountainside, visible only as a flash of light that might just catch someone's eye had they been looking. And as his spirit leaped from one ridge to another, his great paws scattered the dust and pebbles in all directions, as if a powerful whirlwind was skittering down the mountainside.

Reaching the base of the mountain, Karbel streaked across the green valley, leaving behind him just the faintest of paw marks in the long grass. But so slight was his presence in the physical world that the grass soon bounced back into shape, and no one would have guessed that the spirit of the beast had passed that way, hurtling towards the forest to meet, head-to-head, the rampaging spirit that had dared to invade his domain.

It was hard to run when terror held the boys in such a fierce grip. Jack and Cameron found themselves stumbling blindly over fallen trees and broken branches. Some trees had lodged themselves against others, teetering precariously at weird angles, ready to crash down at any second.

"Keep going," Jack gasped, pulling Cameron to his feet as he tripped over a mass of exposed tree roots.

"Was that...? Was it really...?" Cameron stammered, his eyes wild with fear. "How... Jack, I don't understand... How can this be happening?"

"Don't talk, save your breath...come on, Cam, this way." Jack held onto Cameron's arm, half pulling, half running, cold sweat trickling down his back.

But Cameron was rapidly falling apart with fear. "What're we going to do? If it can smash trees to pieces it can smash houses... If it rampages through the village it'll kill everyone... I've got to warn my mum—"

"Cam! Calm down!" Jack pleaded. "We'll warn them. We'll warn everybody. Look, it's heading towards the valley – it's not coming this way. We just need to stay calm, and keep running."

"O-okay!" Cameron stammered.

Jack glanced around as he staggered on, staring in total disbelief at the mayhem left in the wake of the scene they'd just witnessed. He'd always thought ghosts were a joke. Until now, even Cameron had only thought of them as floating, misty images – certainly nothing that could actually do any harm.

Jack's head was spinning. It couldn't have been supernatural, there had to be some rational explanation. His dad would know...

"We'll head back to the site...tell my dad...he'll know what to do."

"Aye," Cameron muttered, hanging onto Jack's sleeve, constantly looking back as they floundered their way through the chaos of destruction. "Your dad will know what to do."

Jack prayed that he would. Firstly, though, he and Cameron had to reach him. The shattered forest creaked. There was a minefield of danger ahead, and an unspeakable horror lurking somewhere behind them. Jack couldn't help wondering if they would actually see his dad – or either of their families – ever again.

Out in the valley, the beast lay in wait. Karbel's keen eyes penetrated the branches at the edge of the forest, watching the path of destruction coming towards him.

Tree after tree came groaning and crashing to the ground. Each time, the thunderous vibration reverberated through his belly. Instinct made him sink low to the ground, ready to pounce, as he would have when he was mortal. Now, the stench of decay grew stronger with every passing second.

Karbel bided his time, waiting to see what demon would emerge from the trees. As he waited for the first glimpse of this evil spirit that was running amok here in his valley, he unsheathed his spirit claws, ready to attack.

Suddenly, he saw it. As a gigantic pine tree came crashing to the earth, sending up an explosion of dust and leaves and debris, Karbel saw the cause of all this destruction.

Its massive shape, outlined by a glowing red aura, was immediately clear to him. Karbel shrank back, hissing, snarling and spitting. A cacophony of emotions shattered his spiritual form so that a myriad of colours and fleeting shapes appeared and disappeared, as anger, hatred, fury and fear flooded through Karbel's spiritual being.

Mammoth!

Karbel recognized it instantly. Just as a human had ended his mortal life centuries ago, so a crazed mammoth had slain his mother and his siblings when he was just a cub – leaving him orphaned.

Agonizing memories flooded Karbel's mind...

He and his fellow cubs had been frolicking with their mother in the long grass. They were familiar with mammoths, they were used to their slow, lumbering ways. They lived in harmony. The danger lay with humans. Humans were to be avoided. But mammoths posed no threat.

Only *this* had been no ordinary mammoth. Karbel's mother had sensed the difference instantly. She had sensed the danger. But there had been no time to lead her cubs to a safer spot in the mountains.

It had charged at them for no reason.

Karbel's mother had leaped to the defence of her babies, but the mammoth had brushed her aside with one sweep of its mighty trunk, and then finished her, along with his brothers and sisters, with a vicious pounding of feet, trunk and tusks.

In terror, Karbel had fled and somehow managed to escape the massacre. But he had grown up an orphan, with memories that still caused him such pain that he would cry out in agony.

But no one ever heard.

Now, as this monstrous apparition rampaged ever closer through the forest, Karbel recalled the senselessness of the creature's actions – and he knew...he knew without a doubt...

This was the very same twisted soul that had wiped out his family.

It had returned.

Had it returned for him? Could this be the reason he had been left on earth, alone – to face the creature that had slain his family, and that would have slain him too?

Well this time Karbel was ready. And with sabre teeth bared, he prepared to pounce.

As the mammoth came blundering out into the open air, Karbel leaped at its glazed, red eyes.

Viciously, his fangs and claws slashed through the searing red mist that surrounded it. He tasted its vile stench.

Startled, the mammoth reared back, trumpeting a shrieking sound that resounded through the valley. Then, as if in fright, it turned tail and fled, lumbering clumsily through the mess of fallen logs, rampaging back in the direction it had come from.

"Did you hear that?" Jack gasped, his chest hurting with the effort of running so fast and scrambling over the catastrophic debris that had turned the peaceful forest into a disaster zone.

"A trumpeting sound?" Cameron whispered, his voice shaking. "Like an elephant's trumpeting?"

"Yes," Jack breathed, looking back over his shoulder. Nothing moved behind them, the gaping corridor of destruction just led back as far as he could see. "Keep running, Cam, don't stop."

His friend clutched his side. "I've got a stitch... can't breathe!"

As Cameron staggered to a halt and gulped in great breaths of air, Jack's eyes darted in all directions, watching for movement through the trees. Nothing stirred, except for the rustle of leaves blown by the eerie draught channelled along the gaping corridor of fallen trees. It was a chill gust, but Jack was sweating and was glad of the cooling air.

"Are you okay? We need to keep moving," Jack coaxed his friend. "Come on, Cam, you can do it."

Cameron raised his head – his glasses were sitting crookedly on his nose and his face was red and sweating. "Tell me now..." he gasped. "Tell me now that you don't believe in ghosts!"

There was no chance to say any more. They both felt the distant vibrations of thudding feet through the ground.

The colour drained from Cameron's face. "It's coming back!" he whispered.

"Run!" yelled Jack.

They fled. Running, stumbling, panic-stricken, falling over the debris, aware that the forest floor was now vibrating again, that piledriver motion hammering the ground once more. *Thud...thud...thud...thud...*

The earth shook. *Thud...thud...thud...thud...* Faster and faster, thundering, pounding, and then a raging, bellowing sound that screamed of another time, another era. A sound that was no longer of this world.

"It's going to kill us!" Cameron sobbed, stumbling again. "It's catching us up."

Running so hard that his legs burned with pain, Jack glanced back and saw, to his sheer terror, a huge, shimmering, red mass powering towards them. There was no time to try and make out its shape, but its immense size was obvious, and the movement left nothing to the imagination. He had seen the lumbering sway of elephants running once, on television. He saw that same motion now, felt each great foot slamming down into the earth.

Thud...thud...thud...thud...

Cameron was right. It *was* going to kill them. It was going to crush them into the ground, like ants.

It's a shame it can't be left in peace...

Jack felt the sob rise in his throat. Ahead, in the distance, he glimpsed the perimeter of the forest, but only open pasture and moorland stretched that way, with no protection at all from the rampaging monster thundering up behind them.

It was closing the gap between them. The smell was back. That vile, rotting stench of decay was cloying his nose, sinking down his throat, so that he wanted to be sick.

"I can smell it," Jack groaned, his stomach heaving.

"You keep on about the smell!" Cameron suddenly exploded, his hands clenched into fists as he stumbled, panic flaring in his eyes. "Smell isn't going to kill us. Its feet and its tusks are what will kill us...flatten us..." He collapsed to his knees.

Jack hauled him up and dragged him as best he could towards a denser part of the forest, where the trees still stood upright. Maybe they could hide...

The vibrations through the forest floor continued, becoming fiercer. Constantly looking back as they stumbled from tree to tree, Jack saw the monstrous red aura closing the space between them. Rampaging, crashing into trees like they were cardboard, flattening everything in its path. Now he could distinguish the glowing outline of its massive head, swaying back and forth, and flashes of its huge tusks gleaming like red crystal.

Thud...thud...thud...thud...

It thundered nearer, the trees offering no shelter, as they were ripped aside by the monstrosity bearing down on them. The boys felt the icy blast of energy overwhelming them, the stench of decay and evil enveloping them, thunderous feet slamming into the ground until they both lost their balance. Any second now it would smash down onto them.

Then it happened. They were both whisked off their feet. The ground shot from beneath them and they screamed in terror. This was it! In a second they would be slammed down and crushed by a massive foot, or feel the agony of a tusk speared through their bodies.

They hit the forest floor.

Expecting excruciating agony, they were stunned to feel a firm but gentle weight pinning them down. Jack could hardly move. Someone's hand was on the back of his head, physically holding him flat against the earth. From the corner of his eye he glimpsed a flash of tartan as the blast of ice-cold energy thundered past them and the stench faded.

"Don't make a sound... Let it go," a voice whispered in Jack's ear. It was such a raw Scottish accent that even Jack could barely catch what he said.

For long, silent minutes Jack and Cameron remained pinned down on the soft, wet earth. Then, slowly, the arms that were holding them relaxed and released them.

They scrambled shakily to their feet in time to see an elderly-looking man bounding over the debris to peep out from behind a tree, across the open pasture.

He was wiry and old, dressed in full traditional regalia – kilt and all – and swinging a walking stick that was as knobbly as his knees.

Jack and Cameron glanced at each other, too stunned and shaken to speak, but utterly grateful for the old man's intervention.

Having checked that the danger had gone, the old man strode back towards them. Although he looked ancient, there was a certain strength to his gait, as if he bore some warrior-like pride.

Jack shook himself – he felt delirious with shock.

"Are ye all right?" the old man asked, smiling, making his face crinkle like corrugated cardboard. His hair was gingery-grey and stuck out at all angles from under his beret. He wore a sash over his shoulder, pinned with a brooch in the shape of two thistles, and his tartan kilt looked weathered and old.

"You...you saved our lives," mumbled Jack shakily. "Th...thank you."

"Och! That's all right, laddies, it's ma job to take care of folk."

Jack couldn't believe how relaxed the old man was. Didn't he realize what he'd just witnessed?

"Although I have to admit, rescuing folk from

evil-minded mammoths is a new one on me." He raised one eyebrow. "But what d'ye expect if ye go around disturbing graves an' awakening the dead?"

"So...so that *was* the ghost of the mammoth?" Jack stammered. "We didn't imagine it? It wasn't an earth tremor?"

The old man gave a little shake of his head. "Do ye really need to ask that question, laddie?"

"But that's not possible. It's dead!" Jack gasped, knowing in his heart that it was true, yet still battling with the insanity of it all. "It's been dead for thousands of years."

"Restless spirits take no heed of time."

Cameron picked up his glasses from the grass. He was shaking from head to toe. "But how can ghosts knock down trees? How can they have all that strength?"

"Ghosts aren't always floaty, misty things with no substance," the old man said with a chuckle. Then his smile faded and he looked steadily at both boys. "Often as not they're as real as you or me. You might almost think they were flesh and blood."

"So what are you?" Cameron demanded. "Some kind of paranormal expert?"

"Och! I've seen many a ghost, laddie," the old man said, cheerfully. "Mind you, I've never seen one that big before!"

Jack couldn't believe how the old man was just taking this all in his stride, as if he came across rogue mammoth ghosts every day of the week. "Have you been helping out at the dig? Only you're not local, are you? We live in Endrith and I haven't seen you before."

"Och no! I've nothing to do with the folk that's digging up the bones. But you'll not have seen me before..." He gazed vaguely away into the distance, then shot a look back at Jack, eyes as bright as buttons. "But I've a wee place right here in the forest."

"I hope it hasn't been wrecked," murmured Cameron.

The old man smiled that crinkled smile. "It's awful kind of you to be concerned, but it'll be fine."

"So, what do you do around here?" Cameron

asked, curiosity overcoming his shaken nerves. "You said it's your job taking care of folks. Are you some sort of forest ranger?"

"You're awful quizzical," the man remarked. "If it were me who'd almost been trampled into the ground by a dead mammoth's big feet, I'd be asking questions like, what are we going to do about settling him back where he belongs?"

"But it's gone, hasn't it?" Jack exclaimed in horror. "You're not telling us it's still around...?"

The man cast him a long, piercing look. There was something strange about his eyes. They were so sharp and alert, and deep too – as deep as a fathomless loch. Eyes that had witnessed more than most, Jack suddenly realized, and as the old man continued to stare at him, Jack felt every hair on his body start to prickle.

Softly, the old man whispered, "When ye awake the dead, it takes an awful lot of rockin' to get them back asleep."

Cameron broke the spell as he asked anxiously, "So, it might come back again?"

"Aye! Where else would it go? The Valley of

Shadows was the land it knew when it was alive. It'll just be out there...somewhere...waiting..."

"Waiting for what?" Cameron's voice was high-pitched. "Waiting for us? So it can trample us into the ground, seeing as it didn't get us the first time round?"

"Aye, you, or anyone else that happens to cross its path," said the old man.

Cameron started to panic again. "We've got to tell people...the police...our parents..."

"I need to tell my dad," Jack added, trying to stay calm.

"Aye, and bring all kinds of folk to the forest, curious to see a ghostie," said the old man pointedly. "And wouldn't it just love that? Lots of living beings to pummel into the ground."

"No!" Jack cried, instantly picturing the scene. Of course people would come, he realized. People would come in their hundreds to actually catch a glimpse of a ghost.

"Listen, laddie," said the old man softly. "What are common folks going to do to stop a raging spirit that's got nothing in its soul except a lust for blood and carnage? If you go running, telling folk there's a ghost of a mammoth, they'll want to see for themselves. They'll not believe you that there's danger – that it can hurt people. They'll want to witness it with their own eyes... and then it'll be too late. It'll likely be the last thing they ever see. They'll no' stand a chance."

"So what do we do?" pleaded Jack. "My dad..."

"Your daddy and all the others that have disturbed its grave would have done well to let it lie in the first place. But it's too late to worry about that now. Nothing of this world can stop it once it's risen – no army, no weapons."

"So what can we do?" Jack cried, feeling utterly helpless.

"We have to reach it on its own spiritual plane," came the old man's answer. "That'll mean we need a priest. He'll need to pray over the grave. He'll need to bless it and sprinkle holy water over those bones." He turned urgently to Jack. "Get him there and don't tell another living soul. There'll be a priest at the chapel, no doubt?"

"Yes – Father Kelly," Jack said swiftly, relieved that there was an answer – that the old man knew a way to send the mammoth back where it had come from.

"We need him. I canna get there maself. You laddies will have to go and get him."

"But you'll come with us?" Cameron fretted. "He might think it's a joke. He'd believe an adult. He'd believe you!"

"I canna leave the valley. It's up to the pair of ye."

"But my dad will give you a lift to the church," Jack said quickly. "You won't have to walk. And we don't have to explain to him about..."

"No laddie...I *canna* leave the valley." His deep, grey eyes locked onto Jack's. "Ever!"

Another shiver ran down Jack's spine. What did he mean, *ever*? He wasn't a prisoner. But before Jack could ask, the old man swung his walking stick upwards and pointed off into the distance with it, reminding Jack for a second of some ancient warrior leading his army into battle.

"You laddies need to go now. Do exactly as I've said, and tell no one, mind. Keep all this to yourselves. Move softly," he added in a hushed voice. "Keep under cover of the forest for as long ye can. Hide and be still if it spies you. Away with ye now!"

He gave them both a push, making them run a few steps. Then Jack halted and called back, "Where will you be?"

The old man had almost merged back into the trees. "I'll no be far away."

"Who are you anyway?" Cameron demanded suddenly. "What's your name?"

"Ma name's Rab...Rab Stewart." His voice drifted back to them through the trees. "Away with ye now. Godspeed!"

chapter six

They kept to the shadows, darting from one tree to another, senses on edge for sounds or vibrations, watching for any sign of movement or destruction.

They spotted nothing. A quiet peacefulness had settled over the forest now that the carnage had ceased. High up in the undamaged trees, a few birds fluttered from branch to branch, and on the ground a rabbit darted from beneath a fallen tree trunk and scurried into hiding amongst a pile of leaves.

They hurried on, skirting the perimeter of the forest for as long as possible before making a run for it across the open land.

"Can you spot anything?" Cameron hissed as they ran on, keeping low.

"Nothing," breathed Jack, his eyes searching for the weird red glow he'd seen as the *thing* came lumbering at them.

"You can't smell it?"

Almost like an animal, Jack raised his head and sniffed the air. "No, thank goodness. It's weird that I could smell it and you couldn't."

Cameron didn't seem to be listening. "We *have* to tell your dad," he blurted suddenly.

"He won't believe us," Jack exclaimed. "Not without seeing for himself. You know what he's like. It has to be cast-iron evidence. There's no way he's going to believe we've seen a ghost."

"Just like you, till a little while ago!" Cameron remarked, casting him a tiny smile.

Jack nodded. "Exactly! He won't take us seriously – especially if we tell him it's the ghost of the mammoth."

"But it could attack at any time. What's to stop it heading back to its grave? Or it might go on a rampage through the village..." Cameron's voice rose anxiously. "I keep thinking about my parents – I have to warn them!"

"Hang on!" Jack cried, recalling the steely look in Rab Stewart's eyes. "I'm worried about my family too – but I reckon the old man knows what he's talking about. I really think we should do this his way. We've got to get Father Kelly out to the grave before we even think about anything or anyone else."

"And if that doesn't work, *then* we'll tell people – we'll just have to *make* them believe there's a danger."

Jack nodded. "Agreed! But we do it Rab Stewart's way first."

* * *

Father Kelly was eating his Sunday lunch when Jack and Cameron eventually reached his home and knocked on the door.

"Well hello, boys." The elderly priest smiled, dabbing his mouth with a napkin. "My, you're looking hot and bothered, the pair of you. What can I do for you?"

"We need your help," Jack gasped, exhausted after the long trek back to the village. "Something's happened, something really weird. You're not going to believe this..."

"The mammoth's come back to life!" Cameron exploded. "You have to come quick. The old man said you've got to pray for it. It's the only way to stop it going crazy and killing everybody!"

"Whoa!" The priest stopped them, holding up his hands, a bemused smile on his face. "Calm down, now. Catch your breath and tell me nice and slowly, who is it that's going crazy, and what have we got to stop?"

Jack took a deep breath. "The mammoth," he uttered. The word – now that he'd actually said it out loud – almost choked him. He repeated it, drumming it into his own head – and hopefully the priest's. "The mammoth! Its ghost has risen from the grave. It was in the forest, it's flattened half the trees – I know it sounds impossible..."

"It nearly killed us!" Cameron cried, grabbing the priest's arm and practically pulling him out of the door.

"Steady on now, boys," Father Kelly said, digging in his heels. "Let me get this straight. You say you've seen the ghost of the mammoth? The one they're excavating?"

"Seen it, smelled it, almost got crushed by it..." said Jack, seeing disbelief in the priest's eyes. "We're telling you the truth, honestly, Father Kelly. We wouldn't lie about this. We're not making it up. It ripped trees up by their roots. It's left a gaping pathway right through to Endrith Valley."

"If it decides to head for the village, it'll trample everyone into the ground," Cameron wailed. "Nothing can stop it. The old man said a priest would have to pray over its grave, that's the only way..."

"And which old man is this, may I ask?" said the priest, still smiling indulgently at the boys.

"His name's Rab Stewart," stated Jack, trying to remain calm. "I've never seen him before, but he saved our lives. He pushed us out of the way of the mammoth – it would have crushed us."

"Rab Stewart?" repeated the priest, rubbing his chin. "That name rings a bell... But, boys, what you're telling me is, well, to be honest, totally unbelievable. Are you sure you aren't getting carried away? Trees have been known to fall, branches do break, and we've had some bad weather recently." He eyed them suspiciously. "Or are you playing a prank, winding me up?"

"No, we wouldn't!" both boys exclaimed at once.

"Are you sure?" he pressed.

Jack turned to Cameron in desperation. "The old man should have come with us. I knew Father Kelly wouldn't believe us."

"Boys, boys," the priest said kindly. "Just wait

a second. Heavens, I've known you both long enough to know you don't usually go around telling fibs. If you say you're not having me on, then I believe you. You've obviously experienced something that's frightened the life out of you..."

"Yes! A prehistoric mammoth!" exclaimed Cameron, his voice rising. "Or rather, the ghost of one."

Father Kelly looked steadily at both Jack and Cameron in turn. Finally he said gently, "And what precisely do you want me to do?"

"Come and pray for it to go away again," Jack said desperately. He realized, suddenly, how little that seemed, compared to the enormity of the monstrous spirit, but what else could anyone do? "The old man said we should fetch a priest. He said you should pray over the grave – pray that it would go back to where it came from."

"You want me to try and lay this troubled spirit to rest?"

"Yes!" both boys answered together.

The priest sighed, reluctantly. "And, no doubt, you want me to come and perform this ceremony right now, halfway through my Sunday lunch?"

"Sorry," murmured Jack. "We wouldn't ask if we didn't have to."

"It might attack again," added Cameron. "No one at the excavation site knows about it yet. The old man told us not to tell anyone but you, in case they went looking and got trampled into the ground."

Father Kelly scratched his greying head. "This old man of yours has a lot to answer for. I'd like to hear more about him. Perhaps you can enlighten me on the way to the excavation site."

"Thank you!" Jack exclaimed, throwing Cameron a relieved look.

The priest indicated that they should come inside for a minute. "You'll allow me time to put my dinner in the microwave for later and get a warm coat on?"

"Okay, but be qui—" Cameron started, but Jack dug him in the ribs.

With another sigh, Father Kelly busied

himself in the kitchen, while Jack and Cameron sat impatiently on the edge of the sofa.

Ten minutes later, they were all in Father Kelly's car, heading for the excavation site. Now they'd got their breath back, the boys went over their story again. But not for a second did the look of doubt and disbelief leave the priest's face.

The only thing he seemed half convinced about was Rab Stewart. "I wish I could recall where I've heard that name before," the priest mused. "He's not one of my parishioners, that's for sure. Oh well, it'll come to me."

There were more cars parked near the excavation site than usual. Jack guessed that, because it was a Sunday, there were more volunteers and onlookers taking an interest. He tried not to imagine the carnage if the mammoth decided to rampage in this direction.

As Father Kelly parked his car behind a line of others, Jack realized it would be best if he and Cam kept out of sight of his dad. "We'll just keep out of the way while you say the prayers," Jack said to the priest as he took his things from the car. "I can't tell my dad yet... Even if he doesn't believe me about the mammoth, I know he'd be straight off down to the forest once he heard about all the damage there, and probably loads of other people would follow him, just like Rab Stewart warned..."

"It's too risky," added Cam. "Jack and I will just hang around here, so he doesn't spot us."

The priest cast a dubious glance first at one boy, then the other. He was starting to look really unhappy about it all. "I'm going to have to speak to your father."

"No! Please don't!" Jack cried, panicking. "I don't want him to get hurt."

"Please, please don't say anything," Cameron begged.

For a moment, Father Kelly seemed undecided. Then he said, "All right, I'll just tell your father I'm here to bless the site – I suppose there's no need to mention your ghost story. No doubt he'll think I need my head examining... Actually I probably do – ghostly mammoths indeed, I've never heard anything so ridiculous."

Looking at all the experts and enthusiasts working away in the crater, unharmed and undisturbed by anything supernatural, Jack suddenly began to doubt that he'd witnessed anything supernatural himself. Perhaps it had just been a freak of nature after all, like a tornado or a whirlwind.

It all suddenly seemed so unreal. He'd never *ever* believed in ghosts. It went against everything he'd been brought up to believe, yet here he was, dragging a priest all the way out here to pray over a ten-thousand-year-old mammoth's bones. His head swam at the craziness of it all.

But if the mammoth's ghost really was out there, he could only hope that Father Kelly's prayers would do the trick.

Suddenly, Father Kelly rounded on Jack, looking him firmly in the eye. "Are you absolutely sure this isn't just some silly prank?"

"No, it's not! Honestly, it's not!"

"Well I hope not, because I've just remembered where I've heard the name Rab Stewart before."

"You have?" said Jack, keen to know more about the old man.

Watching the two boys intently, as if to gauge their reactions, the priest said, "The Rab Stewart I've heard of doesn't exist – well not any more..."

"Well *our* Rab Stewart exists, all right!" Cameron said firmly, his eyes bulging behind his glasses. "If it wasn't for him, we'd both be as flat as pancakes now."

"Yes, so you say," nodded the priest. "So it can't be the same one, can it? The Rab Stewart I'd heard of died at the Battle of Endrith in 1314. He was a leader in the Endmore Clan. Legend has it that his ghost still roams the valley."

Jack and Cameron exchanged glances. "This guy wasn't a ghost, that's for sure!" exclaimed Jack. "He was as real as you...or me..." His voice trailed away as Rab's words echoed through his head...

Ghosts... Often as not they're as real as you or me. You might almost think they were flesh and blood.

"I'm pleased to hear it," Father Kelly remarked, oblivious to Jack's sudden paleness as he humoured them with one of his understanding smiles. "Otherwise I'd be praying for *two* lingering souls. Now if you boys wouldn't mind, I'd like to prepare myself." And taking his prayer book, a bottle of holy water, a bowl and sprinkler, he headed off towards the excavation site.

As he walked away, Jack gripped Cameron's arm. The hairs on the back of his neck were prickling. "Cam...you don't think our Rab Stewart could be *the* Rab Stewart? A ghost... another ghost?"

Cameron let out an uncomfortable little laugh. "Jack, a few hours ago you didn't believe in ghosts at all, now you're seeing them everywhere!"

"Well, the thought that we could almost have been trampled to death by one does tend to change your opinion a bit!" he said, sarcastically. "I mean, what else could that have been? I keep trying to tell myself maybe it was a tornado or... I don't know, something else...but I saw that red aura all around it. It *was* the mammoth, wasn't it? We felt the vibration of its feet, we heard it trumpeting. You think it was the mammoth too, don't you? It's not just me going crazy?"

Cameron swallowed hard and shook his head. "If you're going crazy, I'm crazy too."

"That Rab guy was weird though, wasn't he?" Jack went on. "And how come he was just in the right place at the right time?" His eyes widened. "And why did he say he could never leave the valley – *ever*? That was definitely odd, wasn't it?"

Cameron said nothing for a few moments, but stood chewing his lip thoughtfully. Finally he said, "So, we've got a ghostly mammoth and maybe an ancient old warrior... Y'know what else might be hanging around in the spiritual world?"

Jack stared at him, suddenly knowing exactly what his friend was thinking.

Cameron nodded. "Exactly...the beast!"

Leaving Father Kelly to say his prayers and sprinkle the mammoth's skeleton – and most of the people working in the crater – with holy water,

Jack and Cameron ducked out of sight behind the mobile tea van. Jack held his breath as he spotted his dad walking over to speak to the priest.

"You don't think he'll change his mind and tell your dad what we said about the mammoth's ghost running amok, do you?" Cameron whispered, as they peeped around the side of the van.

"Well, if he does, Dad'll either freak out or send for the men in white coats."

After a few moments' chat, they saw the professor pat Father Kelly on the shoulder and return to what he was doing.

"Dad probably thinks he's a nutcase," murmured Jack, as the priest continued slowly walking around the crater's perimeter, reading from his prayer book and sprinkling holy water over the skeleton.

One or two of the palaeontologists glanced up, looked briefly at each other and then got on with their work.

"They *definitely* think he's a nutcase," Jack murmured unhappily. "If they only realized he was trying to save their lives."

"Yeah, but he doesn't really believe us, does he?" Cameron muttered. "He's only humouring us."

Jack watched miserably. "Do you think it will work if he doesn't really believe in what he's doing?"

Cameron shrugged. "I don't know."

Eventually, Father Kelly walked back to the boys. He looked weary. "There! I've blessed the site, and prayed for the mammoth's soul – if it has such a thing – to be at rest."

"Did it work?" Cameron asked hopefully.

"Everything will be calm again now," the priest assured them, heading back towards his car. "If there was a troubled spirit, it's been laid to rest. There's nothing more for you boys to worry about."

Jack wasn't so sure. "You don't think that we should walk up to the forest, where we last saw it, so you can say some prayers there too?"

Father Kelly was starting to get impatient. "Do you realize how far it is to walk to the forest, young man? Apart from the fact that my dinner is waiting and my feet are wet and frozen, I'm not as young as I used to be." Seeing their anxious faces, he smiled. "Even if we could drive up there, it wouldn't be necessary. There's nothing to worry about, boys. This spirit you think you've seen is at rest now. Come on, I'll give you a lift back to the village."

The priest dropped the boys off outside the chapel.

"Thank you!" Jack called out, as Father Kelly headed towards his house. He gave a little salute in response, before closing the door with a resounding thud.

"What do you think?" Cameron murmured uncertainly, as they walked down the street towards their homes. "Reckon it did the trick?"

Jack wished he felt confident, but all he could do was shrug. "I hope so. We did what Rab Stewart said – what more can we do?"

"So we tell our folks now," Cameron stated. "Jack, we have to. They're going to have to know about our bikes, and the destroyed trees and everything."

"Maybe we should check with Rab first?" suggested Jack, suddenly hopeful that the old man might tell them the mammoth really had gone for good.

Cameron looked horrified. "I'm not going back there, not after what we've been through. How would we even know where to find him anyway?"

"No, you're right. I don't really fancy it either." Jack shuddered at the memory of those pounding feet gaining on them and the vile stench among the trees.

Jack heaved a great sigh. "Okay, let's just tell our parents, and see what they have to say."

"They'll think we're crazy!" Cameron groaned. "No one is going to believe us, are they?"

"They'll have to, once they've seen the destruction in the forest."

"Aye, you're right. Even so, Mum and Dad won't be pleased about my mangled bike. That was my birthday present."

"They should be glad they haven't got a mangled son!" said Jack, managing a feeble smile. "Anyway, Cam, I'll see you later."

"Okay. I'll let you know what my folks say."

* * *

Jack was ready for his parents to be pretty astonished by his story and he didn't really expect them to believe it, but the last thing he thought they would do was laugh.

He stared in horror at the pair of them at the dinner table that evening, as they clutched their shaking sides.

"So that's why Father Kelly was at the site today – you'd managed to con him into believing your little yarn," his dad chuckled. "I did wonder what made him suddenly decide to come and bless the bones."

His mum's laughter faded. "Jack, that wasn't nice to involve poor Father Kelly. He's getting on a bit. He doesn't need to be running around on a fool's errand."

"Mum!" Jack wailed. "It wasn't a trick. You want to see our bikes...they're mangled!"

The professor's face straightened suddenly, as both parents began to realize that their son was deadly serious. "Wait a minute, are you honestly telling us that your bike is wrecked?"

"Yes! Smashed to pieces!"

"And Cameron's?"

"The mammoth's foot smashed down on them both," Jack stressed. "If Rab Stewart hadn't dragged us out of the way, we'd have been mangled too!"

He was finally getting through to them. They both stared at him in amazement, before his mum jumped up and went into the hall.

"I'm going to ring Cameron's parents..."

"Dad, I'm not messing about. It was the mammoth. You have to see the forest – all the trees have been smashed down."

"It's not possible," said his dad, shaking his head. "I'm not saying you're lying, Jack, what I'm saying is that there will be a perfectly natural explanation for this phenomenon you've experienced."

"Natural!" Jack exploded, jumping to his feet. "It was *super*natural!"

"Now, calm down, son. There's no point in getting in a state over this. We'll both go down to the forest and you can show me."

Jack made to head for the door. He still wasn't

keen on going back there at all, but it was the only way his dad was going to believe him. But his dad stayed put, and indicated that Jack should sit down too.

"Not tonight. It's too late. You can show me in the morning, before school, okay?"

"Okay," Jack reluctantly agreed, realizing there was no point in arguing now. It would be too dark to see anything properly anyway.

A few minutes later his mum came back, shaking her head. "Cameron's mother seems quite impressed that her son has such a creative brain! She says he's always had a fascination with the paranormal and thinks this ridiculous story is just the overactive imagination of two lively teenagers. She also said that you both need to remember where you left your bikes and get them back!"

Jack groaned. "Why won't anyone take us seriously? There was a ghost of a mammoth out there. It smashed through the trees, it mangled our bikes, it tossed a full-grown hairy coo right over a wall, and it very nearly crushed Cam and me like ants!"

"Jack, I've told you, we'll check it out in the morning," stated his dad. "If we leave at about seven we should be back before you have to set off for school."

Realizing that this was the best his dad would offer, Jack headed for the phone. "I'll tell Cam we'll pick him up... I reckon his mum ought to come too!"

As it turned out, Cameron's mum said she had no intention of going on a "wild goose chase", but if Cameron could be bothered to get up early, he could join Jack and the professor to pick up his bike, so long as he was back in time for school.

Later that night, as Jack lay in his bed, he couldn't help wondering what would happen if Father Kelly's prayers hadn't worked. The mammoth could rampage all over the Highlands – and then there might not be a school left to go to.

Lying there in the dark, with just a shaft of moonlight filtering through the chink in his curtains, he thought he heard a sound.

The sound of an elephant's trumpeting.

It was a haunting, bellowing sound, drifting on the wind from far, far away...

He pulled the sheets over his head, and prayed it was just the overactive imagination of a lively teenager.

chapter seven

Karbel was guarding the Valley of Shadows. This was his domain. The evil spirit of the mammoth would not be permitted to enter. Karbel would defend his land to the very end.

His spirit versus the crazed spirit of the mammoth that had wiped out his family. He didn't know which was the mightier. Perhaps time would tell.

Karbel had lain in the grass by the forest all day, his yellow eyes focused on the gaping corridor of fallen trees. He was ready to pounce again, if it returned, his hatred growing as the memories of the terrible loss of his family continued to torment him. Throughout the day, he had watched and waited for the mammoth to come smashing its way back through the forest, to try and enter his valley again. Karbel was angry with himself – his vicious attack earlier had seen the ghostly creature off, yet it hadn't been his intention to scare it away. He had wanted to inflict mortal wounds onto its soul, to rip its spirit into such shreds that it would disperse to the four winds. But the monster had simply turned tail and fled.

And he had let it go. But there would be another time, of that he was sure.

Karbel sensed the creature would come back – if only to seek revenge for that first attack.

So Karbel had lain in wait, until the sun had disappeared from the sky and the blackness of night had descended over Endrith Valley. Now a full moon cast its dim light across the mountains and the loch, transforming grey into silver. Nothing stirred.

The mammoth's stench was no longer on the breeze. The chaos of its rampage through the woodland had ended, yet Karbel still sensed its spiritual presence. Waiting for the mammoth to return was making him impatient. And he had no wish to be taken by surprise, as his mother had been, eons ago. He needed to hunt it down... and destroy it.

With the dawn's grey light came the first drops of rain. Karbel slunk forward, his belly close to the ground, flattening the long grass with his shimmering form. He slithered through the undergrowth, through the rain, until he reached the forest edge and the chaos of fallen trees stretched before him.

Raising himself up from his belly, Karbel's sharp eyes focused ahead. The forest was swathed in shadows now, but Karbel moved on stealthily, padding quickly, leaping effortlessly over fallen trees, invisible to the mortal eye but for a shimmering glow darting this way and that – easily dismissed as a mere trick of the light. After a little time, Karbel spotted some objects that he knew to be of human origin. He had no idea what contraptions they were, only that they had been crushed and mangled underfoot. He realized that humans would hate this mammoth spirit just as much as he did.

Reaching the far side of the forest he stood, looking out from the trees. Rain beat down now in torrents, streaking through the early dawn. His gaze penetrated the gloom.

He paused on the skeletal form of the tree that had been struck and burned by lightning. He remembered a time when that same tree had been a mighty oak – before the storm came.

Memories jumped into his mind – memories of being awoken from the deepest of sleeps by the most fearsome storm. Karbel had lain on his high rocky ridge and watched the heavens wreak havoc on the earth below.

So fierce and wild was the storm that Karbel believed it had been sent to lift him up and take him to the place where his mother's spirit rested. He had waited eagerly as thunder exploded and lightning flashed. But he had waited in vain.

A bolt of lightning had suddenly hit the oak tree, causing it to explode into an inferno of violent flames. Torrential rain had gradually dowsed the fire and, finally, the storm had passed. Sunlight had dried the earth, and there Karbel had remained – abandoned to his solitude.

Now, as rain splashed down once more, his sharp eyes peered through the dim early morning light and focused on the red glow illuminating the lightning tree.

He recognized the red, glowing aura at once. It belonged to the mammoth. Karbel instantly flattened himself to the ground, his gaze fixed on the apparition.

The mammoth stood with its head bowed and pressed against the tree, almost as though it were sleeping, its rage vented for the moment. It was as if it had butted straight into the tree, not having the sense to walk around it.

Karbel felt no pity. This mammoth was not

like other mammoths. This creature had been deadly in life, just as its spirit was deadly now. In life it had caused nothing but grief and destruction, bringing death and pain to all who had the misfortune to cross its path – not least his mother and her cubs.

A silent snarl escaped Karbel's lips and fury rose in his breast. He would avenge them...

At seven o'clock that morning, Jack and his dad picked Cameron up from his house. He looked tired, as if he hadn't slept a wink. With his hood pulled down to keep out the merciless rain, he dived into the back of the car.

"Morning," he said, sounding unusually dejected. "Jack was telling me on the phone last night that you find it pretty hard to believe what happened to us yesterday, Mr. MacDonald. Can't blame you I suppose – my parents thought I'd imagined it all as well."

Jack's dad cast a quick glance over his shoulder as they pulled away. "It's a pretty unlikely tale, you have to admit. There's bound to be a rational explanation."

"We didn't make it up," Cameron said earnestly, looking to Jack for support.

"I'm not saying you did. I just think you'll find there's a perfectly logical reason for what's happened. No doubt we'll figure it all out once we get a look at the damage to the forest. That's if you both still want to go. It's pretty diabolical weather!"

"You're not going to believe us any other way," murmured Jack, wiping the misted windows.

"I believe something strange has happened to damage some trees," his dad continued, switching the windscreen wipers to full speed. "But I don't think it's the actions of a prehistoric ghost!"

"It was!" Jack murmured miserably, peering out through the drizzling rain. He couldn't help worrying that the monstrous apparition could still be out there, waiting, if Father Kelly's prayers hadn't worked.

"Anyway, I want to check the excavation site

first," said his dad. "I'd like to make sure everything is in order there. Then we can walk across the field to the forest. I know it's a rotten morning, but I want to see if there are any cracks or subsidence. It could have been another earth tremor that you experienced."

"It wasn't!" exclaimed Jack, frustrated. "In fact I don't think the first one was an earthquake at all," he went on, with a flash of insight. "I reckon it was the mammoth's ghost jumping out of its grave."

"What!" his dad exclaimed, with a hoot of laughter. "Son, do me a favour and stop watching monster movies, would you?"

Casting Cameron a long, hopeless glance, Jack slumped back in his seat. He was wasting his breath. He could understand his dad's reaction really, though. He wouldn't have believed the story if he hadn't experienced it himself. But surely his dad would be convinced once he saw the carnage in the forest.

The excavation site was deserted. Everything looked normal, though it was muddier and more slippery than ever. The bones of the mammoth were still there, shining now that the rain had washed the mud off them. Jack stared at them and shuddered. But at least they hadn't been mysteriously crushed to pieces. Or worse – risen from the dead and turned into a ghostly skeleton that could clank its way around the Highlands.

Professor MacDonald walked around the perimeter of the crater, checking the site. Jack hung back, cold and shivery.

"You can't smell anything, can you, Jack?" Cameron asked quietly, as rainwater dripped off his hood and trickled down his nose.

Jack shook his head. "Nothing but mud, thank goodness."

"Do you reckon Father Kelly's prayers did the trick?"

"I should think so," said Jack, trying to sound positive, but doubting his own words. Would a few prayers really have sent such a powerful ghost back where it came from? An ominous feeling hung like a lead weight around his neck.

At last, his dad came squelching back. "Well,

everything looks normal here, thank goodness, apart from it all being submerged in rainwater. There won't be much work done here today, that's for certain." He raised his eyebrows questioningly at the boys. "So, are you pair ready for the forest now? You don't want to retract your story?"

"No!" Jack answered indignantly. "Dad, I wish you'd believe us."

"Okay, okay, let's get going then," he sighed, striding on ahead.

They followed the route Jack and Cameron had taken on Saturday, along the half-finished road, with its discarded bulldozers, concrete pipes and huge mounds of soil. The compacted earth shone a deep brick red, and their boots slipped in the sludgy wet clay as they walked.

Jack hated the smell of clay and mud. It made him think of the mammoth's grave. In fact, the abandoned diggers brought all kinds of macabre thoughts to his mind. Like this was some big machinery graveyard, where everything had just been left, deserted. Or like some monstrous *thing* had come this way and scared everyone so badly that they'd abandoned their machines and run away.

"It feels weird, doesn't it, Dad?" Jack called out, trying to catch up with the professor. "It's all really silent – I wish there were some people about."

"I do too," murmured Cameron, casting Jack an uneasy glance as he hurried alongside him.

"It's quarter-past-seven on a cold, wet Monday morning," his dad called back over his shoulder. "The only people about are us crazy bunch, going on a ghost hunt."

"Are we really the only ones about?" Jack murmured to Cameron, as they trudged on, trying not to slip over in the mud. "I feel a bit...well... jittery, like we're being watched."

Cameron's eyes darted everywhere. "It's probably just your imagination. Father Kelly's prayers will have worked, I'm positive."

"Yeah, I'm positive too," Jack said, unconvinced. "Only...he said the prayers at the excavation site, but the mammoth's ghost was long gone from there. Do you reckon he should have prayed over by the forest, where the ghost actually was?"

Cameron's eyes looked out anxiously from behind rain-streaked glasses. "Don't know..."

"Cam, I've got a really bad feeling—"

"Don't, Jack! The ghost has gone. Father Kelly did exactly what Rab Stewart said to do!" Cameron interrupted him, as if trying to convince himself. "Come on, let's catch up with your dad."

The boys lengthened their stride, but getting closer up to the professor didn't rid Jack of the eerie sensation that was creeping up his spine. Now, more strongly than before, he felt that they were being watched.

By someone...or some*thing*.

"Did you hear that?" Cameron asked suddenly, looking back.

"What?" Jack turned and stared back the way they'd come, but saw nothing except a wide expanse of wet, red mud.

"Don't know...just...something."

Nerves were getting the better of them both and Jack was starting to feel really queasy, like his stomach was tying itself in a knot. "Dad, I think we should head back to the car!" he yelled impulsively.

"I don't think so, son," said the professor, marching on. "This was your idea remember... Unless you've something to tell me? Like this is all some practical joke?"

"No, it's no joke," Jack promised. "I'm just not feeling too good. I feel a bit sick..."

Suddenly, he shot Cameron a startled look. The smell was back. It filled the air like rotting meat.

The colour drained from Cameron's face. "Ah no! Don't say you can smell it..."

"What the devil is that awful stench?" Jack's dad suddenly exclaimed, covering his nose and mouth with his hand. "I've smelled that before...down at the site when we had the earth tremor. Urgh! That is absolutely vile!"

"It's the mammoth," Jack croaked, his throat so tight with terror that he could barely speak.

"What?" gasped his dad, turning back, his face screwed up in disgust at the terrible smell.

"It's the mammoth," Jack cried, spinning in all directions, trying to catch sight of the glowing red apparition which he knew would be there, somewhere. "It's here! It hasn't gone... Cam, can you see it?"

"Jack?" Professor MacDonald frowned, striding back towards them. "You're worrying me now..."

"Run, Mr. MacDonald!" Cameron suddenly shrieked, shooting off to hide amongst the pyramid of concrete pipes ahead. "Run! As fast as you can!"

Jack moved to run too, but his dad caught his arm and held him fast. "Calm down, son. There's nothing here to be afraid of."

"Yes there is!" Jack yelled. "Dad, it's the mammoth, it's here, it's right on top of us. You can smell it..."

There was a thud, and the ground shook. They looked frantically around, trying to see what had made the ground under their feet suddenly shudder. Jack knew, though. He knew, and the thought terrified him.

"It's real, Dad, it's real! We've got to run...
only I don't know where. I can't see it..."

"Jack, hang on. You're getting yourself into a
real state."

Another *thud* was followed by a quick
succession – *thud...thud...thud...*

The road surface suddenly began to dance.
Massive splashes shot up from the ground, as
gigantic, invisible feet slammed down into the
mud, sending it flying into the air.

"What on earth's happening?" gasped the
professor.

And then they saw it – a faint red aura,
moving, shimmering, glowing. The huge form that
it outlined might have been made out of crystal –
a glistening illusion. But there was no mistaking
the lumbering great shape of a prehistoric
mammoth...coming straight at them.

Its huge, tusked head swayed from left to
right as it rampaged towards them. Hollow red
eyes that glittered with hatred fixed on them with
terrifying determination.

"In great heaven's name!" cried the professor,

as his knees buckled with shock.

Jack grabbed him to stop him from falling into the path of this crazed monster from the past. "Run, Dad, run!" he begged, dragging at him, as the horrendous vision thundered nearer.

It took his dad just a few seconds to grasp the situation. Then, struggling to keep on his feet, he grabbed Jack's arm and they raced down the red clay road, desperate for any sort of cover.

The pile of concrete pipes seemed the only escape and, as the *thud...thud...thud* drew closer, and the stench of the mammoth filled the air, Jack found himself being bundled inside one of them.

Scrambling on all fours, Jack scuttled to the centre of the concrete pipe. He glanced back, expecting his dad to be right behind him. "Dad, get in!" he screamed, but all he could see at the opening of the pipe was a red glow, where his dad had stood just a moment ago. "Dad...no!"

Next came an almighty thud and everything swayed. Concrete ground against concrete and Jack was suddenly toppling forwards, head over heels, as the massive pipes were sent rolling down the hillside. Faster and faster he span, while all around was the crashing chaos of massive concrete tubes colliding with each other. He didn't know if he was upside down or the right way up. Battered and bruised, he tumbled crazily in the rolling, bouncing cylinder, knowing that, at any second, another pipe could come crashing down and smash him to smithereens.

Glimpses of green and sky mingled with flashes of grey concrete. He tried, desperately, to cover his head with his arms, to protect himself as best he could from the battering. Then, just as he was beginning to think the spinning would never stop, the rolling motion started to slow, until it was just his head that was still spinning. All the pipes had ground to a halt.

Everything hurt, every limb and every bone, but at least nothing seemed to be broken. Jack sat for a moment, glad to be alive, waiting for his head to stop whizzing crazily around. Then, slowly and cautiously, he dragged himself to the end of the pipe and peered out. He was in the field. Concrete pipes lay at all angles. A gigantic reel of cable was nearby too, something else the mammoth had headbutted into motion. But now nothing moved. And, as far as he could see, there was no raging mammoth waiting to crush his head with its massive foot.

Then, glancing back, he saw it – the eerie red aura, leaning up against a bulldozer at the top of the hill. The mammoth's head was pressed into the side of the machine, as if it were locked in a battle of strength.

Something touched his hand and Jack almost leaped out of his skin. To his utter relief Cameron was standing there – battered and bruised, but alive.

For a minute, all Jack could do was stand and stare. Then, shakily, he murmured, "You've got a cracked lens." As he straightened his friend's spectacles for him, he felt tears stinging his eyes. "I think it got my dad..."

Cameron's chin crumpled, but determinedly he said, "Maybe not. Maybe he got into a pipe like we did. Come on, Jack, let's try and find him. Maybe he was spun out..."

His voice trailed away. They both knew that if he had spun out, chances were that another pipe would have hit him on the way down. They began their search.

The concrete tubes had scattered over a wide area, some of them landing so they were balanced precariously on top of one another. The boys trod warily, continuously glancing back to check the mammoth wasn't coming after them. But it remained at the top of the hill, locked head-to-head in a clash of strength with the inanimate machine.

"Mr. MacDonald," Cameron called out softly, determined not to dwell on the depressing thought that Jack's dad didn't make it. "Where are you?"

"Dad!" Jack called out quietly, terrified that they might alert the mammoth to their whereabouts and wishing that there was someone around who could help them. "Dad...Dad...where are you? Cam, it's no good, he's not—"

"Jack!" A faint cry came from one of the pipes. "Dad?"

"Jack! Jack, over here!"

Cameron punched the air. "Yes!" he whooped under his breath as they raced to the pipe the voice had come from.

"Dad! Are you okay?" Jack asked, crawling in on hands and knees.

"I think my ankle is broken, son," the professor said, his face screwed up in pain. "Are you both all right? Is Cameron okay?"

"Yes, I'm fine, Mr. MacDonald," Cameron called back. "Thank goodness you are too."

The professor put his arm around Jack and hugged him fiercely. "Son, I'm so sorry for not believing you. I don't know what to say...this is the most stupendous thing I've ever witnessed. It just doesn't equate to anything I've dealt with in all my life..." Lost for words, his voice trailed away.

Jack cast him a little smile. "It's okay, Dad. It's not every day that you meet the ghost of an extinct woolly mammoth!"

Cameron poked his head into the pipe. "The mammoth is making the bulldozer rock back and forth. I think it's going to tip it over."

"Dad, what are we going to do?"

"I can't move, son," the professor said almost apologetically, struggling to get something from his pocket. "I'll ring for help...though heaven alone knows who can combat that thing."

As he pulled his mobile phone from his pocket it fell apart in his hand. His eyes fluttered shut in a gesture of desperation. Then, rallying himself, he said. "Okay... So, we need to think clearly and rationally now. It's up by the bulldozer, is it?"

"At the moment," Cameron reported. "It seems to have forgotten about us for the minute."

"Right! Well, no matter how far away it is, there's no way I can walk anywhere, and I'd just slow you pair down if I tried."

"I'm not leaving you, Dad!" Jack cried, holding onto him.

"You're going to have to," said his dad firmly. "If I'm to get medical help, and we're to get some sort of assistance down here to deal with that... thing...you're going to have to leave me here and run for help."

"How? We can't go back the way we came."

147

"Absolutely not," agreed his dad, his face creasing with pain. "You need to put as much space between you and that creature as possible."

"What do we do then, Dad?"

He thought for a second. "The best way is to go through the forest into Endrith Valley, head around the base of Endrith Mountain and take the little pathway back to the village. You know the way I mean, don't you, Jack? We've walked it once or twice."

Jack nodded, hoping he would remember the way.

"Run home and look in my contacts book for a man called Professor Herring. There's nothing he hasn't studied – including the paranormal. Tell him what's happened. He'll know what to do and he's well respected enough to make the police, army, psychic experts – or whoever – get down here and sort this mess out. And, son..." He grabbed Jack's hand. "Make him believe you!"

"I will, Dad," Jack promised. He hesitated, not wanting to leave his dad all alone. "What about Mum?"

"She'll have to know, but under no circumstances let her come down here. Promise me, Jack! It's too dangerous."

"I promise."

"Well, go on then!" urged his dad, managing a little smile. "Fast as you can, son."

Jack gave him another hug before crawling back out of the pipe.

The rain had stopped now and the mammoth was still thudding its great head against the side of the bulldozer. The boys broke into a run, tearing across the grass in the direction Jack's dad had instructed them to take.

Less than a minute after Jack and Cameron had set off, they heard the awful creaking, crashing sound of a huge piece of machinery toppling to the ground.

Looking back, they saw the bulldozer lying on its side. The glowing, red mammoth stood triumphantly over it, its head raised high, swinging its great tusks and trunk back and forth in manic excitement. And then an unearthly trumpeting bellow rang out across the valley.

Jack shuddered. "It'll be looking for something else to mangle now... Come on, Cam, there's no time to waste."

chapter eight

Karbel had watched the commotion. He had tracked the monstrous spirit, once it had stirred from its place by the lightning tree. He followed its lumbering gait to a hole in the earth where humans had sliced away a great ribbon of grass, leaving a line of bare soil that trailed far into the distance.

There Karbel held back. He had no wish to go

nearer to the place where humans wrought their destruction on the earth, bringing turmoil ever closer to his domain. So, watching from a distance that morning, Karbel had seen the mammoth slam into the humans' strange giant tubes, sending them rolling down the hill. And then two young humans had staggered out of them.

He'd watched them as they ran frantically this way and that. How he hated humans. All peace was being wrenched from his valley. Humans and this crazed spirit were the only troubles to ever blight his existence. They needed to be wiped out, destroyed.

He fixed his sharp eyes on the two young males as they scuttled into the forest. To kill these tiresome humans would be a pleasure – and they would be easy prey.

His natural instinct to hunt excited him suddenly. His mortal desire to stalk and kill was still prevalent – even in death.

It had been a long time since he had tasted warm flesh and his mouth watered at the thought. He would have to summon up all his energies, all his desires, to manifest long enough for the kill, but such a feast would surely restore his full strength for the great battle which lay ahead. The battle between his spirit and that of the monstrous entity that had taken the life of his mother and siblings.

As his eyes locked onto the small, pathetic humans and he breathed in their scent, a deadly snarl rumbled from his black jaws.

But the sudden sound of another human vessel crashing down into the field, followed by the raged bellowing of the mammoth, made Karbel turn swiftly and look back.

He saw the creature's red aura, its trunk and tusks raised high, triumphant in dislodging the massive contraption. Karbel's hatred flared. It was a powerful and monstrous creature – in life and in death. What chance had his mother and her cubs had against it?

What chance had he against it?

Anger shot through his veins with such fervour that, for a brief moment, Karbel took on true physical form. Fleetingly, a real, live sabre-toothed tiger was standing on the Scottish moors for anyone to see. A huge beast with dark golden fur, a rounded belly, and fearsome head – its vicious sabre teeth protruding and curling downwards from its black gums.

Karbel lashed out with his talons – and three deep claw marks ripped through the bark of a nearby tree.

He would have his revenge. And the young humans would be good practice. He would relish the chase, and he would relish the kill even more.

His moment of pure fury passed and Karbel's physical form ebbed away. He turned and bounded towards the forest. He would stalk the young humans in his spirit form, reserving his energy so that he might draw on it and manifest himself once more at the crucial moment – the moment of attack. As he slipped beneath the trees, he licked his lips, eager for the taste of blood, now that the chase had begun.

* * *

"What if this Professor Herring doesn't answer his phone?" Cameron fretted, as they half ran, half stumbled through the forest. "Or what if he doesn't believe us?"

"My mum will be there, she'll know what to do," Jack said firmly, doing his best not to let panic take over and render him useless. He had to think clearly.

"But she didn't believe us before. What if—"

"She'll believe us!" Jack almost shouted, cutting Cameron off in mid-flow. "If we can't get hold of Professor Herring, we'll get the police... the ambulance, the army, even! Cam, we have to think positively. Somehow or other we'll get help... We have to."

"What are the police going to do?" Cameron argued frantically. "They can't kill something that's already dead, can they? Even Rab Stewart got it wrong. He was so sure the priest's prayers would get rid of it, but that didn't work, did it? So who can help us, Jack? Who?"

"I don't know! I don't know!" Jack yelled, panic welling up inside him. "But we will get help, okay? Somehow, we've got to help Dad..." He glanced at his friend as they ran on. Cameron's face was white with terror. Softly, he added, "Cam...it's going to be all right. Now save your breath and keep running."

They raced on, finding a route through the forest that wasn't littered with fallen trees and broken branches, all the while glancing back over their shoulders, terrified in case that glowing red aura should suddenly reappear.

As they reached the far edge of the forest, Jack thought he sensed something following them. Out of the corner of his eye he glimpsed movement – something shimmering far behind, through the trees, like a streak of light. But he put it down to exhaustion, or maybe a bead of sweat that had trickled down his forehead, or perhaps it was just the daybreak glinting through the trees.

There was no red glow, no stench of evil and decay.

They stumbled out onto the grassy expanse of Endrith Valley and stood, gulping down the cool, damp air. Early morning mist still hovered over the grey waters of the loch, so that only the tips of the tall reeds and bulrushes could be seen. They swayed gently, moved by the lapping water.

"Do you think it'll come after us?" Cameron fretted, glancing back through the forest.

"Why should it?" answered Jack, hoping positive thoughts might calm his own fears. "Come on, we need to get a move on. It'll be safer once we reach the mountain. I don't think that real mammoths were mountain climbers, so, with any luck, ghostly mammoths won't be either. If it does come this way, we can climb up out of its reach."

"Good thinking," agreed Cameron. "Nothing can hurt us if we climb high enough."

Endrith Valley was as silent and tranquil as ever, and the boys walked briskly down to the shores of the loch, glad of the white mist to shroud them and the chill wind to cool their overheated bodies.

Endrith Mountain loomed up ahead. It was normally a great place to hang out. There were rocks to climb and caves to explore – or you could just laze about and watch for eagles up amongst the clouds.

The valley looked so normal. It was almost as if Jack's dad *wasn't* lying injured in a concrete pipe at the far side of the forest, and that the ghost of a prehistoric mammoth *wasn't* trying to kill them.

But they both knew that the sense of normality could be shattered at any moment.

"Come on, Cam, keep going, pal..." The words had barely left Jack's mouth when something splashed behind them. Something in the water...

They span round.

"It can't be..." Cameron breathed.

"Don't panic," said Jack, his heart hammering with fear. "It's nothing, just a fish flapping about in the shallows."

"How do you know? What if it's crept up on us?"

"No, it hasn't, Cam, the air smells clean. I'd smell the mammoth if it was near."

Cameron breathed in deeply. "How come the smell thing doesn't work with me? Your dad could smell it too. Your sensitivity must run in the family."

"Must do, I suppose." Jack shrugged.

"Weird though," continued Cameron, as they hurried on, still glancing back. "I'm the one who's always believed in ghosts. You and your dad have always been rational types."

Jack managed to cast his friend a smile. "Well, I believe in ghosts now, okay?"

Cameron nodded. "Aye, and it's good that you can't smell anything nasty now... Woah! What was that?"

Jack felt it too – an icy coldness that suddenly enveloped them, as if the temperature had suddenly dropped by fifty degrees. Then, a second later, a blast of heat hit them, as if someone had just opened an oven door in their faces.

They staggered backwards.

Something was swirling before their eyes, a dazzling whirlpool of light. It flashed and danced, a light mass that had appeared from nowhere and now shot this way and that, changing shape and direction, emitting an icy coldness that chilled them both to the bone.

"What's happening?" Cameron cried, trying

to run. "Jack, what's happening?"

Jack felt as if he was being cocooned in a great block of ice...a moving mass that shone brilliantly, reflecting shades of golden brown, streaks of yellow... Slowly it was developing colour and shape...and definition.

A great blast of heat hit Jack full in the face, sending him reeling backwards, and with the blast came a roaring sound that seemed to have come from a million miles away. A sound not of this earth...

"Cam..." he stammered, but his friend was scrabbling on the ground, trying to escape the swirling mayhem all around them.

The light mass was becoming darker, the streaks of gold and yellow colouring the shifting illusion, giving it substance. And now a more distinct shape was beginning to become clear.

As Cameron scuttled away, the whirling mass of colour leaped after him, giving Jack the chance to see it clearly from this short distance – and what he saw turned his blood to ice.

A beast! A massive animal the size of a lion

or tiger was slashing and ripping at Cameron like he was a piece of meat. Vicious sabre teeth bit down onto his friend, yet it was as if the two were on different planes – the image of the beast wavered in and out of view, like some strange reflection and, try though it might, it seemed unable to connect with the physical world – with Cameron. At least, not yet...

Jack staggered, the sensation that he was going to faint almost overwhelming him. Somehow he stayed focused, somehow he didn't scream in terror. Yet for an instant he couldn't move – he could only stand there, quaking with fear and disbelief.

But with every passing moment the optical illusion was taking on more form, more substance – its colour deepening, those sabre teeth and black talons looking more fearsome by the second.

Now the grass began to fly up as its great paws pranced and sprang. Leaping into action, Jack picked up a rock and hurled it at the beast's head, yelling, "Get away from him!" But the rock simply passed through the beast's shimmering image as if in slow motion, then dropped harmlessly at its feet.

Desperately, Jack reached for his friend, gasping as the intense freezing swirl of the golden mirage swamped over him, as if he was plunging his arm through ice-cold treacle. He grabbed Cameron and hauled him towards him, staggering as the beast turned on him, its massive, shimmering sabre jaws gaping wide over him, like a terrifying hologram. And with the blast of heat that erupted from its gaping mouth came a roaring sound that echoed hauntingly across the valley.

Reeling in terror, Jack clung onto Cameron's jacket as the beast's presence became more intense – less transparent, more lifelike. He dragged his friend to his feet. "Run, Cam, run!"

Cameron was white. "The b...beast... It's manifesting..."

"I know! Just run!"

"Can't outrun it..." Cameron gasped, falling to his knees again.

"You've got to try..." Jack begged, tears filling his eyes... Then something snagged his arm.

Looking down he saw, to his horror, a long rip had appeared down the sleeve of his jacket.

Slowly, he raised his eyes and found himself staring straight into the yellow, slitted eyes of a sabre-toothed tiger.

It was no longer a shimmering light, or a ghostly vision from another dimension. It was real, it was solid.

And it was going to kill them.

chapter nine

There was no point in running. This was a vicious predator, they were its prey. Like cat and mouse. Its eyes were locked onto them. Eyes that were brilliant in their colour and their depth and, for a moment, Jack was riveted by the incredible beauty and power of this long-extinct animal. He could see its muscle structure, the texture and colour of its coat – how it gleamed.

Almost as if time was standing still, Jack gazed at the creature in wonder. Outside of his terror, he was aware that he was looking at a magnificent, prehistoric animal that no living being had ever laid eyes on. Mesmerized, he could do nothing but stare as it opened wide its sabre jaws, preparing for the kill. And, in that moment, he noticed something else.

The smell.

It was back.

So, the beast smelled as rancid as the mammoth, Jack thought vaguely, as this slow-motion film rolled on before his eyes.

It was the same smell. The same vile, rotting smell that accompanied the mammoth. He felt his stomach revolt against the stench. It was worse than before...much worse.

And then he realized why. The smell wasn't coming from the beast at all. It was coming from behind him.

Only then did he feel the massive presence looming towards them. He knew what it was before he even dared look round.

It came at them furiously, its great head swaying from side to side, the glowing red aura changing to a dark brown; its misty outline taking on shape and form, substance...and mortality.

Jack and Cameron could only stare as time stood still. It was no longer an apparition. No longer a ghost. Just like the beast, it was becoming real...

Flesh and blood.

It thundered up behind them – a mammoth! A real, prehistoric woolly mammoth. Its dark brown coat was long and tangled. Its enormous yellowy tusks curved up towards its glazed red eyes. Eyes that speared them with an intense evil, colder than anything Jack had ever felt in his life before.

As it overshadowed them, it raised its huge trunk and issued a bellow that seemed, to Jack, to trumpet the start of a battle.

Cameron clutched at his arm. Jack gripped him as tightly in return as they shrank between these mighty and deadly foes.

Spitting and snarling, the beast coiled back, and then sprang towards Jack and Cameron. With shrieks of terror they ducked to the ground – but the powerful creature leaped clean over their heads. Its target was no longer them, but the mammoth.

The boys scrambled aside, sprinting, terrified, across the rocky terrain to the base of the mountain, where they could hide amongst the boulders and rocks.

Behind them a cacophony of roars and bellows resounded across the valley, like the sounds of hell.

It had almost taken him by surprise, Karbel realized, as he sprang over the puny humans' heads to lash viciously at the demonic monster.

He had been foolish to let himself be distracted by his urge to feed. This was what mattered...

Victory over this monstrosity!

His gaze locked onto the mammoth's evil eyes, power, energy and determination filling Karbel's soul.

The battle had begun.

He would avenge his mother. No matter what it cost him.

Peering out from behind a boulder, Jack and Cameron watched in horror as two prehistoric animals that had long departed this earth became locked in mortal combat.

The beast had already scored its talons across the mammoth's mighty hide, and now, time and again, it renewed its attack, lashing out with its claws, drawing blood with every slash.

Startled by the ferocity of the attack, the mammoth turned and lumbered in confusion towards the mountain. Jack and Cameron scrambled higher amongst the rocks, desperately trying to keep out of sight, as the beast gave chase to corner its foe against the rock face.

Suddenly, the mammoth lunged at the beast, its head lowered, its trunk flailing, sending rocks and stones flying in all directions.

Jack and Cameron tried to keep their heads down. It was agonizing to watch. Could anyone ever have witnessed such a fearsome clash of strength? To Jack, the beast seemed fearless in its awesome rage, as if it was utterly intent on destroying the mammoth. It allowed its massive enemy no respite from its slashing talons – it was everywhere at once, barring the mammoth's way and then leaping fearlessly to inflict more gaping wounds.

Swinging its trunk back and forth, lunging with its great head and tusks at the beast, the mammoth fought back. But the beast was more agile and darted aside, sprinting onto higher ground.

Furiously, the mammoth swung its trunk, trying to dislodge the tiger from its higher vantage point, pounding its huge feet into the ground with rage and sending thunderous vibrations through the earth.

Then, suddenly, the beast launched itself into the air. Black claws unfurled and immediately found their target as they ripped into the mammoth's tough hide. Scrabbling with its back legs, the beast clung on, dangling from the mammoth's huge neck and continuing to bite savagely with its powerful jaws, blood spurting into the air.

Bellowing madly, the mammoth swung its great head back and forth, throwing the beast onto the ground, then instantly raising a huge foot to try and crush its head. But the tiger was too quick for its giant enemy and rolled away.

Jack had momentarily closed his eyes – even though he knew the beast had wanted to kill him and Cam, he couldn't bear to see such a magnificent creature crushed beneath the evil monster's foot. But he opened them again to see the beast still alive and once more lunging to attack.

The beast leaped onto a large, flat rock, and then instantly pounced up onto the mammoth's back, hunching between the giant creature's shoulders, before twisting forwards to plunge its vicious, sabre fangs into the mammoth's throat.

An unearthly bellowing rang out across the valley, as dark red blood spurted from the deadly wound. But as the mammoth's legs began to buckle, it managed to raise its trunk and swipe the beast from its back, slamming the sabre-toothed tiger to the ground.

Before it had a chance to roll aside, the mammoth lowered its head – and lunged.

A fearsome ivory tusk speared the beast through its chest.

"I can't bear it, Cam," Jack cried, turning aside, his eyes burning with hot tears. "They're tearing each other apart."

As more red blood stained the earth, Cameron took off his glasses and wiped his eyes. "They're dying... Jack, look, they can barely stand. The beast and the mammoth are both dying...all over again."

Karbel felt the tusk pierce his body, yet there was no sensation of pain. Instead, the knowledge that he was wounded merely strengthened his desire to rid the world of this monstrous, evil being. Drawing on every last ounce of strength, he struggled to his feet and lashed out with claws and teeth in a final desperate effort, making the mammoth back off, making it stumble.

Relentlessly, Karbel battled on...for his mother, for his brothers and sisters...for himself.

In his heart he was now certain that this was why his spirit had remained earthbound for so long: to await the return of this monstrous evil and destroy it for ever.

Now he would avenge his family. He would not fail. Karbel's determination was fierce, and summoning up his last drops of energy, he loped towards the mountain, clawing himself up the jagged rock face. His thoughts were fleeting...this mountain had been his domain – his home – for so many thousands of years...

He found the ledge, high above the mammoth's head then, gauging his target, he sprang from the narrow ridge and soared magnificently through the crisp morning air to land perfectly on the mammoth's back.

His final bite into its open wounds was fatal.

With its trunk flailing wildly as it tried in vain to dislodge the beast from its back, the mammoth crashed blindly over the rocks, staggering over the grass towards the tall, swaying reeds – stumbling, finally, into the loch.

Karbel clung on, gouging his claws deeper into its leathery neck, refusing to be dislodged. As his sabre teeth continued to rip at the mammoth's throat, the massive creature waded deeper, crumbling from its mortal wounds. Deeper and deeper it staggered, as the water rose higher; over its legs, up to its stomach, lapping over its back.

As the icy water embraced Karbel's bleeding body, Karbel clung on, determined to see the battle through to the end. And as the two great prehistoric creatures slipped from sight, the grey loch waters turned to a sea of red.

The water closed over Karbel's head and he felt the mammoth weakening beneath him. Its immense body shuddered as all mortal strength finally left it. He felt the stark coldness of its carcass – colder than the waters of the loch themselves – before it drifted away. And the stench of evil that surrounded it faded into nothingness, as the mammoth's form fragmented into a million tiny specks of red that quickly disintegrated and were washed away.

Triumphant at last, Karbel felt a great sense of tranquillity and calmness flood through him. He had no desire to swim to the surface, to try and recover from his wounds, yet he seemed to be floating. And there was a strange feeling in his breast. It was a feeling he had almost forgotten... But now he recalled it.

Joy!

He was floating and it felt wonderful. Yet he was no longer surrounded by water. Looking down, the misty loch with its swirls of red was far, far below him. So too were his valley and mountain – his lonely home for so long – all stretched out far beneath him.

He was in the clouds. Floating in the clouds with such a feeling of peace and happiness that he opened wide his sabre-toothed jaws and roared out in sheer wondrous pleasure.

Suddenly, the floating sensation ceased and a gentle softness seemed to lift his paws. He padded through it, delighting in the light, springy sensation. Raising his mighty head, he saw a creature of his own kind sauntering slowly towards him, young cubs following playfully in her wake.

Her eyes were soft, her gentle purr was one he knew so well, and as her warm head nuzzled his, welcoming him home, Karbel felt joy swell his heart and the last threads of loneliness melt away for ever.

chapter ten

Jack and Cameron stayed low behind the boulders for long, stunned minutes, shocked by what they'd witnessed.

Seeing the loch waters change from grey to red, Jack realized the prehistoric creatures would not be re-emerging and, shakily, he got to his feet to gaze out across the rippling surface. Cameron stood beside him in silence.

"Look!" Cameron murmured suddenly. "Look over there, by the forest... Isn't that Rab Stewart? He must have seen the battle too."

The old man was standing there, staring at the water. But then something else caught Jack's eye – a strange kind of sparkling light coming up from the surface of the loch.

He nudged Cameron and nodded towards the tiny dancing particles rising above the swirls of red. "What's that?" he gasped.

"Don't know..." said Cameron.

They watched the mass of tiny sparkles lifting up into the air. In seconds they had gone, but Jack felt the strangest sensation of happiness swell through his body.

Taking a deep breath, he glanced at Cam. His friend was gazing up into the sky and smiling too. Suddenly, Jack snapped back to reality. He gave his friend another, sharper, nudge. "Come on, Cam," he said, urgently. "We've got to get an ambulance out for my dad."

* * *

Professor MacDonald had been lucky – the break was clean and, after a night in hospital, he was allowed home with his foot and lower leg in plaster.

When people saw the destruction in the forest, experts were quick to put its cause down to an earthquake, or a tornado – after all, what other explanation could there be? The fact that nothing registered on the Richter scale, or at the Met Office, was put down to another freak of nature.

Although Jack's mum believed their story, Cameron's parents thought it ridiculous. And, guessing that most people would ridicule the whole thing too, Jack's dad suggested they keep quiet about what really happened. As a respected scientist, the last thing he wanted was for people to start thinking he was some kind of crackpot.

But Cameron couldn't resist telling everyone at school. And whether people believed the story or not, the news got out. Rumours and stories hit the headlines, curious visitors arrived in Endrith from far and wide, and even a television crew turned up.

Jack and Cameron enjoyed being interviewed and showing the TV crew where it happened. Jack's dad, however, managed to keep a very low profile, determined to keep his reputation intact.

Amongst the sightseers who turned up were a group of people from a psychic study society, who were fascinated by everything Jack and Cameron had to say.

It seemed that they had researched rumours of the paranormal in Endrith Valley the year before. In fact, Cameron had read on the internet about one of the women in the group. Her name was Melissa, and she had brought reference books with her, showing sketches of Scottish Highlanders from the past. There were pictures of the warriors of the Endmore Clan from way back in the fourteenth century. Jack and Cameron couldn't believe their eyes when they noticed that the tartan and thistle brooch that Rab Stewart had worn matched the uniform of the Endmore warriors exactly.

Another member of the group said his son, Daniel, had seen the beast too. Some time later, Jack got an e-mail from Daniel himself. He told the amazing story of how the beast had snatched his puppy. Jack was fascinated, and e-mails flew back and forth between them as they related their experiences to each other.

But Daniel wasn't the only one who'd witnessed the beast. After reading the stories in the newspaper, a family with two teenage children returned to visit Endrith. Amanda and Grant were the children whose encounter with the beast had caused such a stir two summers before.

It felt so good for Jack and Cameron to be able to talk about what had happened with others who understood and believed them. They even shared a few jokes about Rab Stewart. Amanda and Grant had met him too, and the four of them argued amiably about whether Rab was really a ghost, or just a knowledgeable old man who happened to be in the right place at the right time.

Life was just starting to settle down again, when the strangest thing happened.

Jack walked in from school one day to find his mum brimming with curiosity.

"You've just had a visitor." She smiled at him.

"Have I?" said Jack, putting down his school bag and heading for the fridge.

"Yes, a funny old chap, very nice though. He came knocking at our door, dressed in all his finery – kilt, beret, everything."

Jack stared at her. Instantly he knew who it was. "Rab Stewart! He had gingery grey hair, didn't he, Mum? And knobbly knees?"

She laughed. "I hardly noticed his knees."

"And he came here? To our house?" Jack frowned suddenly, remembering the old man's words...

I canna leave the valley – ever...

"Yes, it was strange. He looked so out of place," continued his mum. "He was looking at the cars in the street like he'd never seen one before. Anyway, he asked if the laddie whose daddy dug up the mammoth lived here. I said yes, and he said he'd a gift for ye...or rather *you*."

Jack could feel the smile tugging at his lips. "Really? What is it?"

She picked something up from the table and handed it to him.

Jack stared at the two thistles on the brooch and, as his hand closed tightly around it, more of Rab Stewart's words echoed through his mind...

Ghosts... Often as not they're as real as you or me. You might almost think they were flesh and blood.

Jack's smile broadened. "So...he left the valley?"

His mum nodded. "Yes, he said that his work was done in Endrith Valley and it was time for him to go home."

Jack held the brooch tight. He understood. It was over. The old warrior left to haunt the valley after dying in battle seven hundred years earlier could now move on – he could finally *go home*.

The mammoth had gone now, too – except for its bones, which would soon be on display in the Natural History Museum.

And the beast. That magnificent beast, that had haunted Endrith Valley for ten thousand years, was also at peace.

Perhaps it too had *gone home*.

Jack believed that it had.

**Have you experienced the
full fury of the beast?
Don't miss the first two stories
in the trilogy...**

THE BEAST

High on a remote mountainside, something deadly lurks unseen. Something with a taste for blood, from the darkest reaches of time...

Grant can't understand why his sister is so freaked out on their family camping trip. He doesn't believe her story about a monstrous shimmering shape leaping down the mountain. But when he hears the menacing sound of a huge creature stalking around their tent at night, he starts to change his mind.

Somewhere out there, the beast that haunts the Valley of Shadows is gathering strength. Readying itself to attack...

"Evocative and full of atmosphere...compelling and convincing."   *The Guardian*

ISBN 9780746084595

THE REAWAKENING

For thousands of years he has slumbered, dreaming of hunting, killing, devouring. Now his sleep is disturbed. The beast is reawakening.

Daniel's dad is taking his ghost-hunting team to investigate stories of a terrifying beast that supposedly haunts the Valley of Shadows. Daniel goes along just for the holiday; he refuses to believe the rumours. But when the group's paranormal instruments start to shoot wildly off the scale, Daniel is plunged into doubt...and danger.

Could there really be something out there? Are the hunters about to become the hunted?

ISBN 9780746078822

For more terrifying thrillers
check out
www.fiction.usborne.com

MALCOLM ROSE
THE TORTURED WOOD

Dillon is struggling to make friends at his new school and begins to suspect there's something rotten at the core of the tightknit community. He finds refuge in the wood that seems to be at the very heart of the mystery. Will the wood give up its dark secret, or is Dillon being drawn into a trap?

9780746077436

KISS OF DEATH

When Kim and Wes snatch coins from a wishing well in the plague village of Eyam, they also pick up something they hadn't bargained for. As the hideous consequences of their theft catch up with them, their friend Seth desperately hunts for a way to save them from Eyam's deadly revenge.

9780746070642

CHARLES BUTLER
THE LURKERS

"I may not have much time to write this. The Gates of Memory are shutting all around the town. I've been trying not to think about it, trying not to draw attention to myself, but I have to face the facts. Today, while I still know what the facts are. In a few days I may pick up this notebook and not recognize a word I've written. The Lurkers can do that, you know. I've seen it happen."

What are the Lurkers? What do they want? And can Verity stop them?

The Lurkers delves into a nightmare world in the grip of an untouchable enemy.

9780746070659

Andrew Matthews
The Shadow Garden

Matty's sixth sense tells her that Tagram House is harbouring a dark secret. The master, Dr. Hobbes, seems charming on the surface but underneath Matty detects a glint of razor-sharp steel. Her fears lead Matty to the eerie Shadow Garden, and she eventually discovers what's buried there. Now she must untangle the mystery before disaster engulfs everyone.

Like cold fingers reaching from the grave, a chilling atmosphere of mystery and suspense seeps through the pages of this haunting ghost story.

"This is a highly atmospheric novel...a satisfying, gripping read with a truly alarming climax."

School Librarian

9780746067949